Room Meant for Music

Doris Schneider

Cover & interior design: Daniel Krawiec

ISBN 978-1-7333671-1-0

Sable Books
sablebooks.org

Contents

For my students and colleagues at North Carolina Central University.
I continue to learn and to feel because of all you taught me.

Prologue

The present

In the shadows of the cavernous band room, volunteer teacher's aide Ray Nichols searches through a file cabinet of sheet music. She looks for the various instrumental parts of "Pomp and Circumstance" to accompany a very traditional, very Southern high school graduation exercise—busy work to calm her nerves.

She focuses only half her attention on the task; the other half listens to the alternating sounds of chaos and calm between two student musicians and their band director, Allie Nichols—Ray's younger cousin.

"Teacher's aide?" she mumbles. "Ha! Self-appointed bodyguard—that's me—with no idea how to protect Allie from what has panicked her students."

Katie and Marc have convinced their teacher that some disruptive or destructive action will happen here...today. Their source of concern: a combination of videos and photos delivered through an anonymous Snapchat. The images disappeared soon after they were opened, all of them news headlines about school shootings from the past. It began at noon with vague references to "the hot band director and her army of musician minions."

Just to be safe, Allie cancelled rehearsal with a text to all band students, and then left a phone message for the principal.

Katie glances at Marc for reassurance, then reaches into her pocket and produces a gun, a snub-nosed little silver thing—good only at close range, but lethal. She offers it to her teacher. Allie groans as she leans across her desk, head down and shaking in frustration.

"Give me the gun. I'll get it back to your father, Katie. You'll be expelled and probably arrested if it's found on you. There is zero tolerance for weapons at school."

Allie takes a deep breath and slowly releases it. She accepts the gun from Katie and gently sets it on her desk, then slides her hand away, unable to sustain contact with the cold metal. She picks up her long wooden drumstick instead. She strokes it, replacing the cold with warmth and familiarity as she sits.

"I know you did this for me, but you're overreacting. The Snaps may be no more than sensationalism…"

"Sensationalism times ten," Marc stammers. "This isn't Buck. You know that."

Her nerves jangled by the imagined headlines and the very real gun, Ray drops a page of music for trumpet. She watches it wing its way to the floor and settle there. Stooping to retrieve the escaped score, she hears a door open and freezes in her crouched position.

Oh my God!

Oh my God!!!…No one else should be here…not here… not now!

Slowly, Ray looks up, tries not to draw attention to herself, and muffles a gasp when she sees the intruders: two boys dressed in black jeans, t-shirts, reflective aviator sunglasses, and hats pulled low over shaved heads. They stand with feet apart in some kind of television gangsta' pose, each with an arm extended and hand turned, holding a long dark pistol—one pointed at Marc and one at Katie, the student closest to Ray. Allie rises from her chair, and both Katie and Marc automatically move together in front of her, a weak attempt at protection.

Allie grips her talisman—the drumstick.

Everyone is frozen, the next move undetermined. Allie stalls for time with the whispered words she knows will affect one of the intruders. "What's wrong with you, Buck?"

The taller of the two lowers his gun and pulls off his hat and glasses, exposing red-rimmed eyes that blink and seem to have trouble focusing.

"Do you care?" he asks.

The other boy steps forward, swings his gun side to side, and screams, "Where is everyone?" His arm and weapon seem to search for more—more faces, more bodies, more victims to cringe in fear and finally feel his building rage.

"Gone, dickhead," Katie screams back at him. "Rehearsal cancelled!"

The sweeping gun pauses, aimed again at Katie. "Well, then you'll have to do, bitch!"

Buck whispers, "It's over...Let's go."

"Too late," the other boy sighs, slaps his own face as if to wake himself, removes his sunglasses, then laughs as his ultimate decision is made.

Reading his look, Katie dodges to the right, away from the gun; Allie throws her drumstick hard and unerringly at the shooter; Marc bends forward, reaching for the gun on the desk; and Ray leaps from her crouched position—knocking Katie to the floor and covering her.

Buck raises his arm and his gun again.

A shot is fired, then three more fill the room with deafening blasts, the room meant for music.

Chapter One

Twenty-eight years before

Ray loved her cousin from the first moment she saw her, a small bundle handed from the nurse to Aunt Mary's hesitant arms. Ray and her mother leaned forward as sixteen-year-old Mary, too young to be a mother, peeled away the pink blanket to reveal a swollen, bruised face with large bulging eyes, only one of them open. Wisps of dark spiked hair pointed in all directions, and a little mouth quivered as it stretched for a long yawn, then closed again. The one open eye searched until it found Ray and stopped, fixed. From a hole in Ray's chest, an invisible line shot out—an offering—caught in the babe's clenched fist, never to be released.

"Not even!" Mary hissed. "She totally looks like a pirate! Are you sure she's…like…mine?"

"Now, now kiddo," Carla cautioned her younger sister, taking the baby. "Give her a few days and she'll improve. The bruises are probably from forceps."

"I got tired of pushing," Mary snapped defensively. "And it hurt!"

Auburn-haired Carla peered curiously at her sister's infant. She looked for family features as she glanced back and forth between blonde Mary and the dark-haired baby.

"Of course it hurt. That's just the beginning of the burden men dump on us women," Carla snapped as she jerked her head toward her thirteen-year-old daughter, Ray.

"May I hold her?" The young girl pushed tangled hair from her face then wiped her hands on her stained shorts and tentatively opened her arms. Ray carried the bundle across the room, cuddled her first and only cousin, and wondered why they didn't see how much the infant looked like her. Ray's eyes were long and shaped like almonds. The baby's eyes were round. But their coloring was the same.

"Don't you think she sorta looks like me?…We both have

brown eyes and hair." Ignored by the two discussing the horrors of childbirth, Ray whispered praises in the tiny shell-like ears to ease the pain of Mary's harsh words and Mama's harsh scrutiny, the first bumps on her new life's road.

Mary abruptly announced, "I'm naming her Alabama after my...like favorite...like totally radical country band."

Another bump!

Yes, Aunt Mary, Ray sighed in her mind, *totally radical! Alabama Nichols? I hear the clink of rusty, state-issued, no-value Confederate currency. We don't even live in Alabama!*

"What about Carolina or Caroline? After all, we live in North Carolina."

"Nope," Mary insisted, "it's Alabama."

So, before either of them could nickname her Bama or Bam-Bam, Ray said, "We'll call her Allie."

Then she whispered in the baby's ear, "I'm your cousin, Raynelle, but you can call me Ray. We'll be best friends, and we won't have anything in common with those two except our last names."

Mama huffed. "You're giving her up for adoption, Mary. Why are you naming her?...I need a drink! I need two!"

But the new mother was looking at her baby and her be-draggled niece, just a few years younger than herself. In a moment of insight, she knew by the way Raynelle held the baby, she would never let go. After a moment, she said simply, "I've... like...changed my mind."

Chapter Two

Ray became Allie's first and only babysitter. It was spring, and by the time high school dropout Mary was ready to return to her waitressing job, Ray was summer free, released from book bondage to spend the long hot days with her cousin, her new but welcome responsibility.

Allie's face had smoothed, and her hair was tamed. Both eyes opened and shut together but were still unusually large and slightly bulging. Ray thought her beautiful but secretly hoped her head would grow to fit her eyes and wide mouth.

Mama and Mary both worked at the Margaritaville Seafood Restaurant, named for Jimmy Buffett, whose music was played nonstop and who occasionally graced the town and restaurant with visits from his boat. He was the town's only living celebrity. There were many dead ones from the Revolutionary War, the Civil War, the World Wars, and even the movies.

After work, Mama partied with a bottle of vodka and Mary disappeared, partying with her waitress friends, sometimes until the next morning. Mary rarely looked at her daughter, but the small bundle became a connection that drew them all into a rag-tag semblance of a family.

Every morning after Mary and Mama left for work, Ray fed and bathed Allie. Then she carried her outside and intro-duced her to their Southern heritage: the town, the waterfront, and all that lived in both.

Ray was thirteen, too young to drive—even if there had been an extra car. So, she walked everywhere with Allie strapped to her narrow budding chest. They were only a block from the Pamlico River, an estuary where the waters from the Outer Banks met the inland waters from the Tar River, supporting a cultural mix of salt and freshwater sea life in its brackish flow. They fed the seagulls and looked for turtles among the waterlilies in the calm shallow pools beside eroded banks carved out by centuries of hurricanes. Brown pelicans soared past like bomber planes or perched solemnly on pilings. Great blue herons waded in the shallows until spooked by Allie's squeals, then lifted into the air and screeched their own prehistoric complaint.

On one of their walks in town, Ray paused at a historical

marker and read it aloud to Allie. "DeMille Family. Home of motion picture producer, Cecil B. DeMille, and his father, playwright Henry C. DeMille." Walking away, she added, "Cecil B. DeMille is the founding father of the American cinema...and he grew up here. I don't think there will ever be a marker in front of our house saying 'the Nichols women lived here.' Maybe there'll be a sign for you one day...or even me. You know I'm going to college...right after I'm the first Nichols woman to finish high school...and that will not be on the sign." Although she couldn't possibly understand, baby Allie seemed to listen intently to Ray's prattle.

They wandered further down Main Street beside some renovated and some still decaying buildings. "You should know, Allie, except for one burning, this old town survived both British and Union soldiers and was even a stop on the Underground Railroad. I'll explain all that when you're older."

Being outdoors calmed Baby Allie, but patterns in sound and movement gave her joy. Their walks followed paths as random as Ray's footsteps, which sometimes turned into a dance. The music was in Ray's head, a melody no one else could hear. And she moved to a rhythm that no one but Allie shared. That summer the baby felt it through Ray's feet, through music inspired by water, seabirds, and sunlight.

Later, Allie expressed the same unique rhythms with the shakes of her rattle. And when she could sit up, she grabbed anything within reach and hit the floor or her highchair tray like it was a drum.

When Allie could finally walk on her own, it was never in a straight line or even steps. Like Ray, she was bored by the ordinary and predictable. Together but isolated in their shared world, they improvised their way along the waterfront or down a sidewalk. Passersby stopped and stared—beginning the conjecture and gossip that would follow for most of their lives.

They were both labeled "a little nuts." Nuts eventually turned into "crazy" and stuck—with everyone except Will and Ranny, their next-door neighbors.

Chapter Three

Ray met Will five years earlier, when they first moved into the old house inherited from her never-acknowledged father. It was a hot summer day, but Will wore a starched long-sleeved white shirt, khaki pants, and a straw hat. He looked old-fashioned with his carefully trimmed beard, slicked-back hair, and green eyes that saw everything. Like him, his house and gardens were well-kept and beautiful.

He paused, laid down the garden shears, removed his glove, and tipped his hat, "Hello, young lady. I believe you're our new neighbor. My name is William Clayton, but you can call me Will." He shook hands with and spoke to the shy eight-year-old girl like she was an adult.

Emboldened by his friendly directness, she replied. "My name is Raynelle, but you can call me Ray."

"If you don't mind, I love the name Raynelle."

She giggled at his old-fashioned speech and behavior, then took his hand and led him into their dusty old house to meet Mama and Mary.

He was as courteous to them as he had been to her, but Mary drew back and Mama huffed in disapproval.

"Yeah," Mama sneered. "We've heard about you…you two."

"By 'you two,' I assume you refer to my partner, Randolph Keats. He owns the Pamlico Emporium on Main Street. He's also an artist, a painter."

"Partners?" Mama asked. "So, what kind of art do you do?"

"Oh, excuse me. I didn't mean partners in that sense. I am a clinical psychologist. I have an office in my home where I counsel people, particularly veterans who have difficulty adjusting to civilian life."

"Good job?"

"Good enough."

"You might give some counselling to this one," Mama

laughed, nodding at Ray. "She's a little twitchy."

"Twitchy?...in the most charming way possible, I'm sure... Well, I need to get back to my roses. It was delightful meeting you, Miss Raynelle." He briefly bowed to Ray, nodded politely to Mama and Mary, and left.

"Hmmm...I think you just met your first queer," Mama muttered to Mary as she watched him through the window. "Wonder which one's the woman. He seems manly enough... for a queer."

Mary laughed. "Gay, Carla. He's gay. No one says 'queer' anymore. And he's far from my first. But you're right. He is kinda, sorta manly...think I saw him looking at your boobs."

After that, Ray was more careful about inviting anyone into their house.

Will's partner, Ranny (Southern for Randolph), also looked like he belonged in another century. He was clean-shaven, wore his wavy hair long to his shoulders, and like Will, was always perfectly groomed. From the first day they met, he called Ray "Sweetheart."

Will called her "Miss Raynelle" and never overtly tried to analyze or treat her, but he became her most important sounding board about the enormous weights her small shoulders would eventually carry.

Chapter Four

One day in early summer, everything changed. He was unknown to Ray, just a boy in cut-off jeans, a t-shirt, and sockless deck shoes. His hair needed cutting and blew around his face from the breeze that always seemed to flow across the river. He scrubbed the gunnels at the bow of a boat docked at the waterfront. She passed by, in tattered shorts and an old hand-me-down cotton blouse. She pushed back windblown hair with one hand, and cradled baby Allie with the other. A stray dog, as disreputable-looking as Ray, startled her with his gruff bark.

The boy paused, soapy sponge in hand. He looked up through pale hair and lashes. Ray almost tripped. He stared at them. It was a look of surprise and bold recognition. It unsettled her.

Oh my! He's so handsome it hurts. Stop looking at me!

Not knowing what else to do, she lifted Allie's hand to wave to him. His mouth opened in a slow smile as he tentatively waved back. Embarrassed by her ragged attire and lack of personal grooming, she turned her head and skipped away with the laughing baby.

The shaggy old dog followed them home, where Ray asked if she could keep him for Allie. Of course, he became another responsibility for her.

After a bath and brushing, the lab/shepherd/whatever mix of breeds became a handsome fellow, or almost. Mary, self-appointed name-giver of everything, christened him "Old Dog." It fit. She called Ray "Smudge." It fit also and made Ray look more closely at herself.

She began her own regimen of personal improvement: she stole conditioner from Mary, brushed her wild hair into a shiny ponytail, shaved her legs, and wore nicer shorts and tops…at least clean ones.

Ray couldn't stay away from the river but avoided walking by boats where the boy might be working. She wanted to see him but didn't want him to see her, even though, like Old Dog, she'd been groomed into presentability.

One day she risked Mama's response and asked for something for herself. "Boys stare at my nipples when I wear a t-shirt. My English teacher even took me to the side and suggested I get a bra before school starts again. Please, Mama."

Mama laughed. "All you got is nipples. Maybe you'll need one by fall. Stop wearing t-shirts."

But, to Ray's surprise, Mama called a waitress friend. After her evening shift, she brought home a hand-me-down bra that her friend's daughter had outgrown. The daughter was one year ahead of Ray and a gossip. So, everyone would know whose bra she was wearing—and that it was too big. She tried it on in the attic bedroom she and Allie shared. Definitely too big! She discreetly stuffed the B-cups with a little tissue and posed provocatively for drooling Allie.

"Just call me shape-shifter, shape-shifter, ba-ba-boom!" she sang as she swung her hips and tried to shimmy her enlarged chest.

Allie rewarded her with a belly laugh.

Ray had learned to expect criticism and so feared the mysterious boy's judgement of her new and enhanced self. She watched him from a distance and tapped a rhythm on a piling with a piece of driftwood to entertain Allie. The baby's squeals were sometimes louder even than the marina traffic and poorly-tied boats that knocked together in the sunny afternoons.

Ray liked it best in the early evening after Allie was in bed, when she could walk on her own to watch the sunset. The boy would be gone for the day, and she could wander the waterfront, unafraid of confronting his intense blue eyes. She read the names of the boats and tried to imagine where they had been and under whose care. She liked the old wooden vessels best, knowing their stories would be longer and perhaps include a series of different captains, each with adventures worthy of novels.

As she walked, she dreamed that she sailed with the boy to faraway places. And she dreamed that he held her hand. She could almost conjure him into reality, feel him at her side, touch his hand. Almost.

Chapter Five

On a hot noon day, Ray sat on an old piling and closed her eyes as she sang a nursery rhyme to the babe in her arms. A cooling breeze lifted tendrils of hair that had escaped her ponytail as she escaped the moment into a daydream. Below her dangling feet, Old Dog sat up and barked. She opened her eyes in alarm to find the prince of her fantasy standing next to her high throne. He offered a hand of friendship to the protector who did not defend her but wagged his tail in delight.

"I see you cleaned him up," the boy mused.

"Uh, yes…Is he y…yours?" Ray stammered, horrified that she might have stolen his dog. "I mean, I thought he was a stray."

"No, not mine, but I fed him. Then he stopped coming around, so I thought someone else must be feeding him."

In the awkward silence, she said, "Oh!", surprised and charmed by his European accent.

More silence, then he gestured to Allie, asking almost shyly, "Is that Mary's baby?"

Shocked, she stammered again, "You…you know Mary?"

"We were in a few of the same classes. But then she dropped out," he said and nodded at Allie.

"Oh!" Ray whispered, unable to vary her responses. After another silence, she slid from the piling, and Allie squealed with the action, waved her arms, and laughed.

"My name is Hans." He smiled. "I know your name is Raynelle. I asked. And I learned that you are Mary's cousin. So, I added two plus two."

"Did you get four?" she giggled, confused that he had asked about her, that he knew her name. Immediately she wanted to take it back.

What a dumb thing to say! And why would this boy notice me or ask about me?

"I did," he responded, as if she weren't acting like the

biggest dork in town, "…get four, I mean." His speech was different from most American teens, more than just an accent, almost too correct. "What is the baby's name?"

"Alabama Nichols."

"Alabama," he whispered as he felt the name on his tongue. "May I hold her?"

And that's how it began. Hans found them at the piling almost every day at noon and spent his lunch hour with them until Ray had to take Allie home for her nap.

He liked to talk about himself, or so it seemed, and she wanted to hear it. His parents and grandfather had moved from Germany to Canada, where his father died of a cancer identified too late for treatment. His mother wanted to live in a small town on the water in a warmer climate. On their way to the Outer Banks, they drove through little Washington, liked what they saw, and stayed.

His grandfather cleaned boats to feel productive and to teach his bookworm grandson about the sea. There was enough life insurance and saved money for the family to live conservatively, but even his mother insisted on working and was hired as a clerk at a downtown jewelry store. His family seemed to be defined by their work ethic.

Hans often asked questions about Ray's family and herself, but she was too ashamed of their shabbiness, the lack of fathers in their household, the lack of promise for their future, the lack of ethics—work or otherwise. Consequently, she told him very little. He didn't flirt, and they never touched, although she still longed to hold his hand.

Because her own father left before she was born and then died a few years later, she was most interested in Hans's stories about his father.

"Do you miss your dad?" she asked in innocent curiosity.

He looked at her sharply. "Of course I miss him. Don't you…I mean…?" And then he lost his words, remembering the bit of information she had shared. She had never known her father. "Yes," he continued, "I miss him every day. I think it's harder for Mother. She works because she can't bear to be alone."

My father is dead too, but no one misses him.

For a moment, she felt regret.

The summer was long, but not long enough for Ray. As the days shortened, she felt an uneasiness, knowing school would take him away, would change everything.

In the fall, she rarely saw Hans. He was a senior and she a freshman. Their paths rarely crossed. When she did see him, he was with the senior beauty queen, Marissa Meadows. Ray hated her. She tried to focus harder on schoolwork and on Allie, but the image of Hans always slipped in behind her eyelids and interrupted every quiet moment.

In October, she turned fourteen and, although still slim, had found the curves that had been missing. She no longer needed to pad her bra. Boys still ignored her, but older men began whistling when they saw her on the street. Her face always flushed with a combination of embarrassment, contempt, and pleasure.

Then Hans and Marissa broke up in early spring, and he often ran into Ray in the hall or waited at her locker. Their friendship took up exactly where it had left off. One afternoon, near the end of the school year, he walked her home.

At the house, they sat on the porch steps because she wouldn't invite him inside, too ashamed of their "not even good enough for the Salvation Army" home decor.

It was a pleasant spring day, and they both leaned back on their elbows. Comfortable in each other's company, they enjoyed the late afternoon sunshine. Hans shared his dream of the future, of becoming a doctor, the universities he had applied to, and the one from which he had received early acceptance. Her heart ached at the thought of his moving so far away, but she was determined not to show it.

He asked questions about Allie, and for once Ray could respond without feeling self-conscious.

"She doesn't walk," she said. "She hops." This brought peals of laughter from him, and she tentatively joined in.

Suddenly, Mary emerged from the house like a storm and rushed past them, slammed the screen door and all but threw a screaming Allie into Ray's arms. She climbed into her old Mustang, slammed that door as well, and backed out, almost hitting a passing car.

Ray comforted the crying toddler while Hans sat forward uncomfortably. "Did I cause her anger?" he finally asked.

"No, Hans. She's just crying because Mary frightened her."

"I meant Mary."

"Mary? No, she's maybe late for work because she didn't know I was home. Does she even know you?"

"Well, no...not really." He ran his finger gently along Allie's cheek. She stopped sobbing and looked up at him, then hiccupped. He opened his hands to her, and she reached for him.

He held her close and she smiled, laying her head trustingly on his shoulder. They sighed together. Allie released the last shudder of fear at her mother's rage, and Hans made a decision.

"Does your mother think I'm too old for you? I'm eighteen now."

"What?...I mean, uh...I don't know. I'll be fifteen before long...I mean, like...next fall."

"Do you have a date for the prom?"

"Me?" Ray asked, as her cheeks turned pink and her heart paused. "No."

Chapter Six

The disastrous prom and its aftermath changed the course of Ray's life. The school year ended with Hans's graduation and his move to Boston. Ray lived in her attic room—a recluse—until Mary pulled her out of hiding and into her world.

"With the right clothes and a little makeup, you could pass for sixteen or seventeen, maybe even eighteen now that you've got boobs. Here's a skirt and top of mine. Put them on and leave your hair down. That ponytail makes you look twelve. And don't call me Aunt Mary anymore."

"What should I call you?" Ray asked holding up the short skirt and crop top that would expose most of her body.

"Try 'girlfriend.'"

Ray became Mary's wing-girl. Only three years apart, they were more like sisters or friends than aunt and niece anyway, but they were polar opposites. Mary found pleasure in being the center of attention. To become that center, she used her talents for humor and sexual charm. Ray shrank from all attention, even kindness.

In order to survive the negative attitudes that surrounded her at school after the prom, Ray became a ghost. She slinked from classes to home, rarely made eye contact, and focused on her grades.

But Mary did not allow the hangdog attitude to last. She dragged her reticent niece to parties until Ray actually became sick of her own behavior.

One night, a boy sat beside her, carelessly draping an arm over her shoulder.

"Hey there. My name is Johnny. You're too cute to sit here alone. I know how it is. I'm kind of shy myself," he whispered, his breath smelling of alcohol and weed.

When he tried to kiss her, Ray pushed him away and got up and crossed the room to the bar, where bottles of various spirits waited. She picked up the closest one and poured some into a glass.

Two other boys came up and started a conversation. She controlled her repulsion at the taste of the tequila, laughed at their silly stories, and downed four shots before a third boy grabbed her hand and pulled her to the center of the room where several couples danced.

She stood for a moment and then closed her eyes and found the beat. She slowly began to move and to release the sadness and modesty that had been trapped inside for so long. She danced for hours—until Mary enlisted the help of a friend to take her home.

Ray saw Mary as pretty, sassy, and fun—if sometimes embarrassing. She saw herself as plain, awkward, and shy. And she was done with that.

I have a choice. I can be miserable in Mary's shadow...or I can join her.

Mary had introduced her to the bad boys and the good drink, and with the help of both, Ray learned how to laugh too loud, to dance without constraint, and to fantasize that each attentive boy was Hans.

And she did get their attention. Her newfound loss of inhibitions was tempered by a sadness easily mistaken for maturity. The combination made her seem more complex and interesting than Mary had ever been. And although she never saw herself as pretty, the boys and men did.

Neither of them was old enough to drink legally, but Mama drank secretly, hiding booze around the house. It was easy to find, easier to drink.

Unable to trust her mother with Allie when they went out for an evening, Ray took her to Will and Ranny. They had an antique baby bed that actually rocked. Allie loved it and went quickly to sleep with only one story, either read to her or created on the spot.

"So, Sweetheart," Ranny asked one evening, "where's the party tonight?"

"I don't know. Mary finds the parties. I just go along, but I do my homework first."

"Nice trick—if you can keep it up." He paused a moment and sighed. "Mary's only eighteen, but she has truly been around and knows the score. You're only fifteen…and most importantly, you aren't Mary."

"I know. I just need to get out of my own old skin. Mary helps."

"I hear a lot of gossip at the Emporium. We worry about you and who you're trying to become. We (and I include Allie and Will in this) love you the way you are—in your old skin—without the conscious effort to emulate Mary."

"Thanks for your concern, Ranny, and thanks for looking after Allie again. I'll pick her up in the morning so you don't have to wait up tonight."

Mama drank her vodka or wine and watched the two teenagers. She assumed Ray was taking on all of Mary's bad habits. She loved her sister but considered her to be a lost cause. On the other hand, she had plans for her daughter, her Raynelle.

Chapter Seven

One day Mama found a pack of Virginia Slims in Ray's purse.

"You're grounded, young lady. That's my one big rule: NO SMOKING!! My mother, your grandmother, died of lung cancer." She made a big display of throwing the cigarettes into the trash. "That's why you never knew her. No leaving the house except for school—for a month!"

Offended that her mother had gone through her purse, Ray responded with silence. She knew Mama had been proud of her good grades and appreciative of her effort to keep their shabby home clean and for the hours she spent with Allie. She had never expected praise but was hurt by the sudden loss of trust.

Mary found and retrieved the cigarettes. She had borrowed Ray's purse and left them in it.

"Sorry, girlfriend," she said as she passed Ray in the living room—on her way to a party.

The next weekend, after Mama passed out, the two of them dropped Allie at Will's and went to a fraternity bash in Greenville.

When Ray began dating, her mother's suspicions grew, partly because the boys who asked her out were not college-bound "nice" boys. Their lack of manners and respect tightened Mama's jaw until Ray feared her teeth would crack.

The distrust made her feel guilty, even when there was no reason. One Saturday Ray innocently sat on the couch next to Eric, a semi-regular date. Mama walked into the room. Ray jumped and moved away from him, her face flushing pink—as if they had done something wrong. And it felt as if they had.

"Get out!" Mama barked. And he did. Ray followed. After that, they sat in his car and she let Eric do all the things she was sure her mother believed they had done all along. But she pretended he was Hans.

The tension grew, and Ray started to act like a typical sullen teenager. She fueled the fire of her mother's expectations... and lived up to what her mother suspected.

One warm day, Ray passed through the kitchen to the back door in a bathing suit. She didn't notice Allie sitting on the floor under the table, playing with a doll.

Mama had been drinking and slurred her words when she asked, "Where are you going dressed like that?"

"Swimming or posing for a centerfold—haven't decided," was Ray's smart-ass mumbled response. She thought her mother was too drunk to hear or to process her words.

In Mama's mind, the only thing bad as smoking was back-talk. Before Ray knew what was happening, Carla grabbed a rubber flyswatter with one hand and Ray's arm with the other. She smacked her daughter's bare legs with that flyswatter, leaving imprints of it and large pink welts from ankles to thighs and even on her arm and back. She was almost sixteen, too old to spank. She felt beaten instead...and humiliated.

At first, Ray tried to run, but was held by Carla's grip. She stopped, jerked her arm free, caught the end of the flyswatter in her fist, and stood her ground.

"Stop, Mama...before *I* hurt *you*."

Ray's threat surprised them both. It was only then that Carla realized Ray was angry enough and big enough to accomplish her threat. Or maybe she had just sobered up enough to know what she was doing. At any rate, she stopped...and never hit her daughter again.

Ray would have left home that day, except who would have raised Allie?

They never made eye contact after that. Ray didn't want to look at her mother. Until then, she had called her Mama. After that, she was Carla, and all trust had vanished on both sides.

Chapter Eight

At Allie's two-year-old wellness check, Mary complained that her daughter didn't walk right. Dr. Bernstein asked Allie to hop forward and then backward. As he watched, she spun around and then did a funny jumping dance. Mary huffed her irritation.

He asked Ray to call Allie and then closely observed as she walked, an occasional skip in her step. When Allie reached her, Ray caught her up in her arms, praising her. The pediatrician smiled broadly and shook his head.

"She is exceptionally coordinated," he told Mary. "My son is a little older and walks into walls. He trips over his own feet and isn't close to being able to skip."

"Is he a moron?" Mary rudely asked.

"Nope, he's a normal two-year-old."

"If she's so coordinated, then why doesn't she walk like other kids?" Mary demanded.

He shrugged. "I'm not musical. But I would swear she is moving to some kind of music or beat—something in her head, perhaps from a different drummer."

Ray's mouth fell open. He understood.

Mary stormed from the clinic like she wanted to give her daughter back—get a refund or a better kid—but instead was stuck with the defective and irreparable model.

At the car, she whirled on Ray with an accusatory look. "Did you conspire with him on that?"

Ray shook her head, amazed that Mary was actually serious. Mary jerked open the car door and got in. She started the car and drove a half block then backed up much too fast and stopped.

Ray and Allie covered their giggles as Ray buckled her into her car seat. Allie had already learned to accept her mother's lack of acceptance, to smooth the bumps with laughter.

At home, Carla soothed Mary's complaints. "She'll grow out of it. Raynelle did."

Ray left the room.

I have not "grown out of it." I have simply learned to control my feet to avoid criticism, especially yours.

Chapter Nine

While Ray was in school, Carla and Mary worked alternate shifts at the restaurant so one of them could be at home with Allie during school hours while the other was smiling and scraping for tips. It was easy for Mary. She could charm female as well as male customers and make belligerent customers wish they could take her home with them. Carla was less consistent with smiles and made the belligerent customers want to leave and never lay eyes on her again. She was tired of it all, especially the pretended cheerfulness. Carla had played this game of work and childcare and no change or relief in sight since she entered puberty.

When Carla was fifteen, her chain-smoking mother had already spent long months lingering in the pain of lung cancer. It didn't stop her smoking. When she finally mercifully passed, Carla's inheritance was the continued care of her two-year-old sister and an alcoholic father with no income and a foul temper.

The day after her mother's funeral, Carla and her sister Mary caught a bus from their textile town in Virginia to Wilmington, North Carolina, where an aunt lived. The bus terminal teemed with young people leaving for spring break. It was a college town on the southern coastline.

She found Aunt Jean's house, but a stranger opened the door. He sent her to a cemetery not far away. With more help, they found her headstone above a plot where she had been for three years.

"Well Mary, I guess we're on our own," she said to the toddler, who plopped on the ground—hungry and tired—and began to wail.

"We'll go to the beach," Carla offered as she picked up her sister.

She had little money for food but noticed that many restaurants had "help wanted" signs in their windows. Spring break caused a dearth of waitstaffs but an increase in customers. As the student employees from Wilmington fled the town, students from other schools flooded in for a week at the beach.

Afraid of losing her sister and herself to Social Services, Carla responded to the first offer of food, shelter, a job, and kindness. It came from an older man named Bob. He was the cook and temporary manager of a seafood restaurant while the owner was away on a European vacation.

"You look young. Ever waitressed before?"

"Yessir," she lied.

"Who's the kid?"

"My little sister. She's no trouble. She can sit in a booth."

"Booths are for customers. Damn! You're probably both trouble. But you're tall and pretty. You'll pass. The dinner rush is about to start, and I'm desperate. There's a cot in my office. Put her in there and then shadow old Sally until you get the hang of it. I'll pay you next to nothin' by the hour. So, smile big for tips."

"I got the job?"

"You got tonight. Get dressed and get busy."

He handed her a too-tight t-shirt with the restaurant name on it and showed her to his office where Mary was settled with her stuffed bear and a small box of juice.

Bob had an apartment above the donut shop next door. When it became clear after the restaurant closed that she had no place to go, he allowed them to stay with him—just for spring break. And he expected favors in return. A week became a month and then three. When he found her throwing up in the bathroom and too weak to work, his kindness ended. He gave her enough money for an abortion and abandoned Wilmington and them.

Her trust in men gone, Carla had used the money to rent a trailer and buy enough food to get by while she found permanent work and a friend also in need of childcare. She watched Mary and the friend's toddler while the other girl worked and vice versa. Six months later, Raynelle was born. Carla located Bob and wrote, telling him he was a father, hoping for some child support. She never heard from him.

Now that there were three children to watch, Carla was too tired to give much individual attention to baby Raynelle. She also resented the cost and effort an unwanted child brought to her barebones home and budget.

Raynelle was treated like a doll by the two older girls, played with and fought over part of the time, and ignored the rest of the time. She survived, but instead of their treatment turning her into a fighter, she became shy and reclusive, hiding from the other two and playing with the books and toys they had discarded. Surprisingly, in spite of Carla's lack of attention, Raynelle adored both her mother and Mary.

Almost eight years later, a letter arrived. Carla ripped it open and after reading it, sat in the nearest chair.

"Oh, my Lord," she muttered. "He's dead."

"Who?" Mary asked, grabbing the letter from Carla's shaking hands. "Papa?"

"No! Our papa's been dead for years. I just never bothered to celebrate…It's Bob, Raynelle's daddy."

"You got a letter from a dead man?"

Raynelle walked quietly into the room and sat down. She had been listening through the open door.

"No," Carla responded. "It's from a lawyer. It seems Bob died and left a will leavin' everything to me."

"What's everything?" Mary cautiously asked. "A mean dog, a bunch of bills you can't pay, WHAT?"

"A house in little Washington—that old town on the river, near Greenville."

"We been there?" Mary asked.

"No, but I've heard of it—heard it's dead, too. Well girls, that's the leg up we needed. We're movin' to little Washington."

"I got a daddy?" Ray asked in a small voice as the other two jumped up and down in delight.

"No ma'am, you got a house. He actually left it to you, but I'm your mama, and I'll be in charge. If it's awful, we'll sell it and buy something else. Can't be worse than this dump."

In fact, the house had looked to be worth less than the narrow lot it sat on, but there was no rent to pay, and the taxes were low. Selling it would not bring enough money to buy something else. There was furniture, but it was as decayed as the house. So, disappointed but resigned, they moved in. Ray was thrilled.

Mary was almost twelve, able to get babysitting jobs for extra money, and Ray was eight, able to take care of herself and to help with cooking and cleaning, always looking for a way to win her mother's approval.

The newfound freedom allowed Carla time to hang out with the girls at her new job, the Margaritaville Restaurant. She partied and began to experience the youth she had missed. She was only twenty-four. Somewhere between twenty-four and thirty, she became a barely functioning alcoholic.

By the time Ray was a senior in high school, still grieving for her lost chance with Hans, Carla was a missing-in-action mother—unaware of anything except her anger at life's unfairness and her need for another drink.

Chapter Ten

For Allie's fourth birthday, they planned her first ever party. Ray bought balloons and a gift and made arrangements at McDonald's for a group of ten. Mary was supposed to send invitations to six young guests. There weren't many families with small children in the historic district, so the list included age-not-necessarily-appropriate kids belonging to waitresses at the Margaritaville Restaurant.

On the morning of the party, Ray found the invitations still sitting in Mary's room, on the table beside her bed.

"WTF, Mary! You didn't invite anyone to Allie's party?"

"What? I thought you did that."

"No, I did everything else! You're at the restaurant every day. All you had to do was hand them out."

"Oh, boo-hoo! Poor you."

Allie walked in on quiet feet, her eyes large and brimming with tears she tried to hold back. "It's okay. I just want to be with you guys anyway. What does WTF mean?"

Ray threw herself into a chair and Allie rushed to her, wiped away her unshed tears and climbed onto Ray's lap. "Could we ask Will and Ranny to come?" she pleaded.

"It's kinda short notice, but…okay. We can try." She knew they would have trouble refusing Allie, so Ray handed the phone to her. "I'll let you talk to them."

"Sure," Will responded, "what time?"

"Now," Allie giggled, "at McDonald's."

"Ohhh…okaaayyy. We might be a few minutes late…need to stop by a store on the way."

"They're getting me a gift," Allie whispered to Ray who took the phone.

"Sorry for the short notice, Will. You two are the only people she wanted at her party."

"Let me guess. We were the only two invited because some-one forgot to invite kids."

"Unfortunately, true. You're the best. See you at the golden arches."

Carla begged off with a hangover, reducing the party to five. "I could use a drink myself," Mary complained.

"I found a bottle of wine in Carla's closet," Ray whispered, fearing Mary might back out as well. "We have a few minutes."

A short time later, Ray wrestled the purple balloons into the trunk, and then buckled Allie into her booster seat. Mary got behind the wheel.

"You okay to drive?" Ray asked.

"Sure." Mary fiddled with the radio while she pulled onto the street. Ray was lost in thought, and Allie was hitting the car window with her toy drumstick.

The after-work traffic was heavy for their small town, so Ray lowered the volume of the music, hoping Mary would focus on the road rather than the lyrics.

"What's your problem, can't think about Hans with all the noise?…When are you going to let that go? He was always out of your league."

"Shut up, Mary!"

Five minutes later, they still argued, when Allie screamed and threw her drumstick into the front of the car. Mary hit the brakes…then hell happened.

Allie would forget the time that followed, not because of her head injury, not because it wasn't memorable…but because Ray willed it. She had always wanted to protect her from nega-tive realities, wanted her to feel safe and loved.

Ray, however, would remember the crash, would relive ev-ery moment of it every day and every night. Each event of her existence became chronicled as "before" or "after" the crash.

It shouldn't have happened. None of it. A driver on the other side of the road fell asleep at the wheel and crossed two lanes of traffic, drifting into theirs. Ray later learned he was almost home after a long trip with no stops to rest. He was almost home—almost safe. It shouldn't have happened to him or to them, but it did.

Most of all, she remembered the earsplitting reverberations: the screech of tearing metal, Mary's scream, Allie's cry, and a roar like a tornado that tried to pull her out of her seat. She thought she would burst into a million pieces from the sheer ferocity of the sound. It would have been easy to let go and enter the tornado of sound, escape the torture. But she held on.

When the quiet found them, broken only by Allie's sobs, Ray surprisingly felt no pain. The car was upside down. Mary was unconscious. Unable to rouse her, Ray released her own seatbelt, righted herself, and moved into the back to Allie. She calmed her crying and helped her out of the booster seat, eased her down, then crawled behind her through the open window of the crushed back door. As she focused on forward movement, Ray reached around Allie and brushed away broken glass in her path.

When they were clear of the car, a young boy ran to them and picked Allie up. Other cars pulled over and people milled around, shouting, afraid to come closer. Allie turned in the boy's arms and looked at Ray, a lump growing on her temple. "Don't leave me," she murmured and reached out. Then she looked up and saw a purple balloon rising in the sky and reached for that instead. The boy carried her away to a grassy shoulder across the road. Ray watched until she knew Allie was safe, then found she was unable to rise, unable to return to help Mary.

The car was on fire, and before Ray could call out or crawl in that direction, it exploded.

Heat and energy passed through and around her as she flew backwards, landing face down. Gradually, a tinkling and then sharp, bright notes reached her consciousness as debris struck the road in a disharmonious rhythm. She listened, strained toward the music, struggled against the darkness.

Unaccountable time passed. The pain found her. They were in an ambulance. The lump on Allie's head was even larger, turning blue. She suddenly stopped breathing. With all the will-power Ray possessed, she set her own pain aside, held Allie's hand, and prayed for the first time in her life. Her mumbled, fumbling prayer became a conversation with God. Like all sinners in a crisis, she offered an exchange, and struck a one-sided bargain. The monitors alerted the medic and brought him to Allie's side, but before he could administer aid, Ray saw Allie take a deep breath.

Chapter Eleven

Most blamed the other driver for falling asleep at the wheel; Carla found the empty wine bottle and blamed it; some just called it bad luck. No one blamed Mary.

Raynelle put the blame where she felt it belonged—on herself. It seemed like all her life she could have or should have done better. If she hadn't found the wine, Mary's reflexes might have saved them all. She might have accelerated out of the sleeping driver's path, or Ray might have grabbed the wheel and turned their car, missing the direct hit. If she had not found the wine…if she had not argued with Mary and ignored Allie…if it had not been a four-year-old's birthday—a four-year-old with a toy drumstick.

It was a surprisingly difficult decision for Carla to cremate the still smoldering remains from the wreck. Although their decaying house was narrow, the backyard was deep, and thanks to a natural fence of overgrown camellia bushes, it was private. She scattered Mary around the large magnolia tree where Allie's tire swing hung.

Like a thief, I have stolen the love of your child and stolen a life. If I had insisted on driving because you drank most of Carla's wine, you would be alive in my place.

Ray wondered if it was awful or perfect that Allie's playground was veiled with the ashes of her mother. For many sleepless nights she sat in that swing, talked to Mary's dust, shared the thousands of sweet and funny stories about her daughter. Occasionally, Carla staggered out to the porch that wrapped their old house and muttered about the past as she stumbled across the yard to a low crumbling stone wall.

"'Member that old goat, Bob?…Funny, I actually wished he was my daddy 'stead of my man…He was kind…But he was too old—didn't want to be tied down with a toddler and another baby on the way. Hell, I was just a kid myself…I guess most men would run."

She would sit on the ancient wall made of ballast rocks salvaged from the shallow water where ships used to toss them out when they came into dock, lightening their load and emptying their storage to make room for goods to take to other colonies.

She rubbed the stones as she thought about the past, but she never noticed her daughter in the swing on those dark nights. Ray was the unwanted, ignored child for Carla just as Allie had been the unwanted, ignored child for Mary. So, the tall, broken woman spoke only to her dead sister, the one she had sacrificed her youth to protect. And Ray felt the slight all the way down to her damaged limbs.

"You were a good girl, baby sister...even if you were a fool."

Ray picked up her crutches and painfully made her way back to the confines of the house, fleeing Carla's slurred complaints.

Allie's head trauma had required emergency treatment to stop the swelling in her brain, then only rest. But Ray's injuries had been worse: broken ribs and fractures in her right leg and foot. There was no explaining how she had helped Allie, much less herself, from the upside-down car. So, she didn't try. The ribs healed on their own, but several surgeries on her leg and a thigh-to-toe cast limited Ray's movements and her escape from self-imposed guilt and grief.

She and Allie both had trouble moving, putting one foot in front of the other. And it was more than physical damage that caused their paralysis. The house that Allie and Ray had once filled with music and laughter was still and dark. Even Old Dog was depressed, rarely rising from his mat. Who knew Mary's irritatingly demanding personality would have been so important...would be so missed?

Allie wandered the house, looked behind doors and into corners, as if searching for something. She asked Carla where a neighbor's dog was. Her aunt explained that he was gone to a better place. She wouldn't use the word "dead." Allie asked daily about other missing objects, animals, and people but never about her own mother. The stock answer continued to be "to a better place."

Finally, one day she whispered, "What happened to my

purple balloon?"

"Your what?" Carla asked.

Ray answered. "We had purple balloons in the trunk of the car…for her party. She's just trying to make sense of it all, Carla. I'm sorry, Allie, but the balloons burst in the trunk after the crash."

"Oh," she responded. "I thought one got away. I wondered if it went to a better place, too."

Ray held her arms open and Allie walked into them. She stopped asking about missing people and pets and balloons. To avoid brutal reality, Ray perpetuated the "better place" myth. It became a difficult habit to break. She wanted to protect the four-year-old from grief. And she thought maybe Carla was right. Perhaps they were in a better place.

Carla hid losses from Allie with lies; she hid them from herself with alcohol.

Ray wore her sorrow like Dolly Parton's patchwork coat, each remnant representing a different poor choice that had led to the crash and destroyed her family.

It would take years of recrimination and a psychology course for Ray to learn about survivor's guilt. Knowing didn't help. Her self-esteem slid into a puddle at her feet and stayed there—like a shadow that lived in the dark and grew larger in the light.

Chapter Twelve

After the accident, Carla stayed drunk for days, another reason for Ray to miss classes and exams in order to take care of Allie. After all, she just followed the family tradition and became another high school dropout. That was the final blow to her self-esteem.

Will came regularly to see Allie. She took his offered hand, and they went to the river. He used the opportunity to get her to talk about her feelings. Ray needed the same words, but her physical injuries were limiting for what seemed an endless time. On a return home one day, he found Ray on the porch and sat beside her while Allie went inside for juice and cookies.

Ray stuck a twig inside her cast, trying to scratch an itchy spot.

"If that breaks off inside the cast, you might have trouble getting it out, and it isn't clean," Will warned. "A wire coat hanger is also dangerous. It can scratch you, but at least it's cleanable and won't break."

"Hmmm. Good idea. There's probably one in my attic bedroom which I haven't seen in weeks. I sleep in a chair downstairs these days. Whoop-de-doo!"

"Is that sarcasm, Miss Raynelle? Actually, I have a thin wooden back scratcher that would fit inside the cast and wouldn't hurt you...So, what's on your mind?"

"Shouldn't I be on the couch?"

"Well, then I'd have to charge you. Why don't we just talk as friends?"

"Actually, I've been thinking about choices, about all the options of what we might do or say. It seems that life—every day—is an unending series of choices."

"In a way," Will agreed. "But you can't take credit or blame for every choice you make as it might have been influenced by someone else's choice."

"Exactly. Someone else's choice can make my path detour,"

she added and pointed at her cast, "and change lives forever. So, it doesn't matter how many good choices I've made. Someone's else's one bad choice can eliminate all that I have tried to do or be."

"And there's another choice. You can choose to let that defeat you, or you can learn from it and move forward, make better choices because of it."

Tears welled. "Mary doesn't have any more choices. If there is a God, why did he/she/it let that happen?"

"He/she/it?" Will laughed. "God isn't a person, certainly not an it. Did God cross two lanes of traffic and run into your car? Did God make Mr. Masters fall asleep at the wheel? We aren't puppets, Raynelle. We make choices. And if someone else's choices mess with ours, what do we do?"

"We learn from it and move forward, make better choices."

"Good girl. That's called 'free will,' by the way."

"I thought you didn't believe in God."

"I don't care for organized religion—completely different issue. However, that's just another choice. I think everyone has to make their own decision about that one—and about their concept of God."

"So where is she, Will? Where's Mary?" Ray cried.

"I don't know—other than in your memory and heart. If we knew—really, irrefutably knew—it might affect all the choices all of us make. Open your mind, Raynelle. There's more than Heaven, Hell, or Nothingness."

"Sometimes I think Hell is right here, and Nothingness would be a great escape."

Troubled by the implied wish for oblivion, Will patted her hand. "Remember, Raynelle Nichols, your cousin—Miss Alabama Nichols—needs you. Mary didn't save her from adoption, and you didn't save her from a burning car to just leave her behind. Wait here…I'll go get that back scratcher."

Chapter Thirteen

Weeks later, without warning, Hans drove up to the house. Ray stayed in the attic room she had finally managed to get to without falling down the stairs on her crutches. She silently waited while he knocked on the door, praying he would leave. Carla, who had rarely left her bedroom since the accident, finally went to the door and stepped out onto the porch in her nightgown. They sat together on the porch rockers.

Carla didn't invite him in. After a while, she rose and went inside. Hans walked from the front to the backyard. As the attic was the full length and width of the house, with windows on all sides, Ray furtively limped with the help of one crutch, from window to window, watching. He wandered up to Allie's tree. After a moment, he sat in the tire swing. Her heart contracted as the familiar ache of regret washed over and around her. Hans leaned his head against the rope and the tire slowly turned.

She hadn't seen him in three years but had followed the events in his life. She knew his grandfather had died and that he was in Boston, in a premed program. She wondered if he too wished that they could leap back in time, start over. But she had learned that do-overs are few and far between, a distinct lack of "reverse gears" in life.

Carla opened the back door and Old Dog walked outside with Allie. The beloved family pet recognized Hans and wagged a tired tail in response to a familiar touch. Hans opened his arms, and Allie climbed onto his lap, turned and leaned back against his chest. The tire slowly began to spin. They both tilted their heads up to stare at the vortex of white cloud and blue sky, twisting and blending. They both smiled. If only she could join them there, push them on the swing, begin again…But she couldn't, even if she weren't stuck in the attic, wedged in by damaged body and soul.

Allie looked up to the window and waved to her. Ray stepped to the side so Hans wouldn't see, then folded into herself, clearing out the images from which she felt so overwhelmingly excluded.

Chapter Fourteen

Carla had developed a sort of smile that Ray didn't understand, clearly saying "I've got a secret." The smile irritated Ray beyond belief. She wondered if Carla had actually had a stroke that froze her mouth into the sneer-like grin.

Carla had always been a drinker, but usually at home or out with friends in the evening. After Mary's death, she visited the only bar in town during the day and staggered home at closing, visible to all the chatty neighbors. At least she didn't hook up with another drunk and bring him home. In Carla's reality, even when under the influence, men were never to be trusted.

Someone called Child Services. Small town. A social worker called Carla.

"Ms. Nichols, I am aware of your family tragedy, and I am sorry for your loss."

"Thanks," Carla slurred.

"…But…there have been complaints, and if I come to your house for a visit, I suspect I'll be forced to place your niece into the foster program. So, I'm giving you fair warning: sober up, or you'll lose her, too."

Carla resisted the profanities she wanted to throw at the unfeeling, interfering bitch. But she'd heard the words "foster program" and "lose her, too." She finished the bottle of vodka on the kitchen counter, threw it into the yard of the neighbor under suspicion for snitching, and the next day she joined AA, totally hungover.

For some reason, maybe moral support, Carla dragged Allie with her to the first meeting. Ray tagged along out of curiosity. Carla wore jeans and a purple sequined t-shirt, a birthday gift from her waitress friends. Ray wore her usual blue cotton shirt and the only shorts she could get over her cast. Allie sat with her sad face, pulling at the hem of her too-short skirt. She kept looking sideways at Ray, her eyes larger than normal, mystified by the contradictory emotions of the AA members, ranging from tears to laughter. Ray soaked it up, all of it—a reality show better than anything on television.

They had been late and missed the opening formalities. This group (the first of many Carla eventually attended) met in a large Sunday school classroom of the First Baptist Church. Bible quotes and children's drawings decorated the walls. There was a big coffee pot and plates of store-bought cookies.

Allie sneaked curious peeks at the other members, and Ray did the same. They were quite a mix: men and women in business clothes; tattooed bikers in leather; construction workers still wearing their tool belts; teenagers in shorts, high heels, and too much makeup; old women in shorts, high heels and too much makeup; and ordinary-looking folks.

Among the thirty-three souls present, there was also a wide range of skin tones: blacks, whites, browns, and everything in between. It was clear to Ray that addiction was a leveler. There was no advantage to wealth, power, education, or race.

A short, sweaty, middle-aged man in a suit stood and announced, "My name is Ralph. I'm an alcoholic."

"Hello, Ralph," everyone responded.

"I've learned two things in this program. Number one— there is a God; number two—he's not me." Everyone laughed. "Oh, and number three—I keep forgetting number two. That's all I've got."

The group responded, "Thanks for sharing, Ralph."

The woman next to Carla elbowed her and whispered. "He'll probably fire someone when he goes back to work—just to feel all-powerful." She sat back and then moved close again. "At least he won't go home and smack his wife. Sally Nabors has learned how to dial 911."

Ray overheard. *So much for anonymity.*

A tall, lanky, tattooed man in jeans and a tank top stood, gave his name, confessed to being an alcoholic, then continued, "I am here by the grace of the Great North State. In other words, I had a choice between jail and AA." Everyone laughed. "Now I like it when the gals hug me—and so forth," he added, winking. "But I don't want none of that so-forthin' with the guys. That's why I chose AA." More laughter. "I never thought this would be a place where I could tell the truth and people would smile 'stead of shamin' me and would encourage 'stead'a leavin' me. So, I'm givin' it my best shot—one day at a time. That's all I got."

A young Mexican man in office attire stood up and said his wife saved his life when she kicked him out. He'd been sober for five years.

An overweight man in rumpled clothes stood up and angrily confessed that he had been on a three-day binge. Then he paused, turned around, and walked/stumbled out. The man who had chosen AA over jail followed him.

Does he want to drink with him, or talk him out of drinking?

Ray hoped for the latter.

There was a long silence before a young woman stood and gave her name. Her shoulders slumped and her eyes were nearly swollen shut from crying. She had an infant in a stroller beside her. Hesitantly, and with such remorse that Ray's heart broke for her, she told her story.

"I was dry for a month and proud of myself. My husband drinks some, but never around me. Last night, I walked into the kitchen just as he closed an upper cabinet we never use. After he went to bed, I pulled up a chair and found an almost-full bottle of scotch." She paused to regain her composure. "I don't even like scotch. But I drank it—didn't stop until it was all gone… and didn't call my sponsor until this morning. My husband says I want alcohol more than I want him…or my baby. I don't know what to do." Nearby women rose and hugged her.

Carla squirmed in her chair. Like the young wife, she appeared tortured and hungover. Ray hadn't really looked at her mother closely in ages. She had thick auburn hair, long almond-shaped green eyes, and high cheekbones. She was still under forty and, in spite of that snarky secret smile and her hangover, she was still pretty. When she truly smiled, which was rare, it was like a burst of sunshine, easing and blurring those hard lines. Ray suddenly realized, with more than a little irritation, that except for the difference in hair and eye color, they looked very much alike.

There were several veterans of AA who had been in the program and sober for many years. They too rose and told their stories, often with humor, always with sincerity.

When there was a long silence in the meeting, Carla stood and said, "I'm Carla...I guess I'm an alcoholic. I've been drinking for years...It seemed like I had more responsibilities than I could face sober—or at least that was my excuse...I lost my little sister a short time ago, and I guess it has made me go over the edge...I've been on my own since I was sixteen..."

Using her crutches, Ray quietly left the room. It was enough that she had to relive the accidents—her birth, Allie's birth, and the car wreck—in her own head. She couldn't listen to Carla tell their stories or use those three tragedies as excuses for drinking. She waited outside, where many congregated before and after the meetings to smoke. She guessed they could only be expected to kick one habit at a time.

Sobriety for Carla was not instantaneous. It took numerous falls off the proverbial wagon, a series of frustrated sponsors, several support groups, and a trip to rehab that they couldn't afford. Then one morning as they sat in the kitchen, Ray tipped her own chair back on two legs and hoisted her smelly casted leg onto the table—partly to get relief from its weight and partly to annoy her mother. Allie came in, a finger twisted in Old Dog's fur and her thumb in her mouth.

She walked up to Carla's chair and crawled onto her lap. Old Dog laid at their feet. She held Carla's face between her two small hands and looked square into her bloodshot eyes. "Aunt Carla," she whispered, "please stay sober. We need you."

Carla surprised them both by leaning forward and kissing Allie's forehead as she set her on the floor. Then she slammed her fist on the table, unbalancing Ray's delicate position. As her daughter fell backwards, her cast bounced up and Carla caught it, stopped her fall, and lowered her foot to the floor—all in one smooth movement.

Ray was stunned.

Who is that superwoman, and why had I forgotten her powers?

Carla never took another drink. Ray was impressed with her mother's ultimate strength at resisting alcohol, but her ass and legs also remembered Carla's strength. Worse than physical punishment was the force of her words when she lashed out with her laser tongue, when she demeaned and dismissed her daughter. But all that was before Ray stood up to her, before she stopped calling her Mama, before the crash.

She wondered if it was possible that they had begun again: new choices, new challenges.

Chapter Fifteen

Without alcohol to blur things, Carla's awareness sharpened, and her concerns for Allie's adjustment to her losses led them to a psychologist and then a psychiatrist. Sobriety had brought awareness of the way other children treated Allie. They called her "crazy" and distanced themselves, isolating her.

Will, a successful clinical psychologist, had been giving Allie free grief counseling on their walks. But, although Carla had finally accepted Will's overtures of friendship, she could never approve of his lifestyle, and that somehow prevented her from crediting him as a professional. She looked for "real" help elsewhere.

The new psychologist made a big fuss about the way Allie walked. She had been walking with skips and hops since the age of one, years before the accident. So, Carla took Allie's hand and left, calling out, "She hears a different drummer, you fool!"

The psychiatrist prescribed antidepressants and another psychosis medication. Raynelle showed Allie how to fake the act of taking them in front of Carla. She didn't need mind-altering drugs; she needed time and love, and preparation to defend herself against the taunts of other children. Public school loomed in the near future, and bullies were already being formed by narrow-minded parents.

Carla looked at their life and wondered how to normalize it, how to help Allie "fit in" with the children she would encounter in kindergarten.

Her AA group emphasized the importance of a higher power in an alcoholic's life. She interpreted that to mean religion, which to her meant the dreaded church. But she knew most "normal" families in their town were religious. So, she inquired about houses of worship where they all might fit—in other words, where compassion might trump judgement.

Her new sponsor attended an off-the-usual-track holy-roller, speaking-in-tongue, of-no-specific-denomination house of worship.

Allie was dressed in jeans and an old blue t-shirt of Ray's that went to her knees. Carla had woven her ward's dark hair into a French braid which she then fastened with multiple colorful barrettes. Her own ensemble included slacks, a cut-off t-shirt, and a high curly pony tail. Ray thought they looked only slightly mental. But it was easy for her, finally out of her cast and using a cane, to dress in similar old clothes with her long hair tied back by a ribbon. Apparently, Carla had been warned against overdressing.

The service took place in an old building that once housed a Food Lion grocery. Signs for meat, poultry, bakery, etc. were still in place and designated the geography of the once bustling food business. It was now filled with folding chairs and a podium with a painted cross that redefined the old store as a soul business.

As usual, they were late and had to sit in Produce while the minister stood in Dairy. They received curious looks from the multicultural flock of exceedingly well-dressed believers. It seemed pretty ordinary until the minister led them in prayer. As his voice rose and fell in a sing-song pattern, the congregation closed their eyes and began to whisper to no one in particular, then raised their arms, and finally, their voices.

Ray didn't understand a word of it and felt a little uncomfortable until she noticed Allie. Her sad face gone, she beamed with delight, clapped her hands in that special beat of theirs and sang sounds as unintelligible as the others, but in the high-pitched, joyful voice of a child.

Worshipers around them came out of their semi-trancelike state and moved aside, gave her room. Allie saw that as an invitation to dance, and she did. The preacher called to her, motioned for her to come forward. As she danced, jumped, and hopped her way to the podium, the others imitated her movements and the sounds she shouted. But theirs were not the same. Theirs morphed into familiar sounds from their youth, a slightly different rhythm and tone that called even to Ray. She had no choice but to join in with an equally enthusiastic smile on her face. An echoing cacophony rose to ear-splitting heights. They no longer spoke in tongues; they instead created a poor imitation of Louis Armstrong and Ella Fitzgerald scat.

Mortified, Carla stormed forward, grabbed Allie, and ran out of the Food Lion frenzy. Ray followed, dancing with her cane, and shouting praises to God—in the language of jazz.

Later that day, they visited Will and Ranny. Allie told them all about the grocery church (as she called it). Will tried to control his reaction, but Ranny was on the floor laughing, probably picturing Carla's reaction to the whole unique scene.

Ranny preferred the traditions and pomp of the Episcopal church down the street, but Will had no trust or respect for organized religion. After he said as much to Allie, she loudly whispered in his ear, "They don't seem very organized." And Ranny was laughing again.

The next Sunday, Allie attended the Episcopal church with Ranny, and Ray returned to the grocery church alone. She preferred the simplicity, the opportunity to praise her higher being in her own language without regard for the traditions of the more sterilized versions of Christianity. She did not deny in her mind that the other members of the Food Lion flock were communing with their god in a tongue beyond her understanding. But she chose to sing her own sounds and lose herself in an altered reality where she felt the presence of an unnamable and undefinable spirit.

After the service, she always wandered out to the waterfront to meditate alone. She still had not formed an image in her mind of God, couldn't buy the idea of an old man sitting in the clouds, deciding who would live and die and when. She searched for God there beside the boats, in the water, on the wings of seagulls, and yes—even in the clouds. When she closed her eyes and held her face up to the warmth of the sun, she found a loving omnipresence everywhere.

One Sunday, when Ranny was in the hospital with pneumonia, Ray saw Will in her grocery church. He stood at the back, and his eyes were closed as he communicated with whatever deity he could accept. She suspected he might be offering God a deal in exchange for Ranny's safe recovery. She remembered her own prayer after the crash.

That may be the most repeated prayer in history, maybe even prehistory.

Ranny recovered—by the grace of God, or modern medicine, or both.

Chapter Sixteen

Because of the crash and advice from the psychiatrist, Carla had not enrolled Allie in preschool until after the winter holidays. Ray begrudgingly accepted that she needed the interaction of other children, but tears streamed down her face as Carla drove Allie away in her nearly new first-day-of-school clothes. Nothing in her outfit matched in color or style. She did not look "put together"; she looked "thrown together." Ray guessed Carla would simply drop her off. She had wanted to come along, to walk with her to her classroom. But Allie had told her to stay home, that she was four and a half and could go to school alone.

When she returned that day, her knees were bloody, her clothes torn and dirty. She said she had fallen. Ray had a mental image of her being shoved down and kicked. But the next day, Allie once again pasted on a smile and refused to let Ray go with her.

Where does she find that bravery? And at what age does bullying begin?

The memory of Mary bullying her in that trailer where she had been born slowly trickled into her consciousness, and she shuddered.

Ray had already taught Allie to write numbers and the alphabet and to read all the words in her picture books. Allie was quickly moved from preschool into kindergarten. Ray didn't know if it was because of her skill level or simply to protect her from the other four-year-olds, but she was relieved. The five-year-old kids were kinder, or at least they left Allie alone since she was so little and maybe was of no consequence to them. At any rate, she came home each day intact but lonely, in need of Ray's company.

Allie's need was Ray's excuse to remain available to care for her rather than herself.

Chapter Seventeen

Like Allie, Ray had never fit in with groups of people her own age. She was drawn instead to old folks, babies, and dogs. She wandered the neighborhood daily, lost without the child who had been her primary companion for so long.

After Allie's birth, Ray had rushed home from school each day to take over her care so Mary or Carla could return to the restaurant for the dinner shift. One of them worked the morning shift and one the lunch. Now, with Allie in school and Mary gone, Carla had no reason to work split shifts. She stayed home during the day, read magazines, slept, and attended AA meetings. Then she worked the dinner shift when the tips were greater. Consequently, Ray stayed away from the house during the day—until it was time to meet Allie and walk her home.

A real job that paid money was still out of the question for Ray. It seemed natural and necessary to maintain an independent schedule in order to be available for Allie after school. In the mornings, she volunteered at the nearby hospice center, comforted and calmed the dying, and helped the trained personnel, mostly doing the work they abhorred. But, as a volunteer, she could set her own hours.

One day a girl with a backpack full of books joined Ray as she walked beside the community college.

"What's your major?" she chirped.

"Um…undecided," Ray responded, too embarrassed to admit to being a high school dropout.

"Mine's English Lit. I plan to be a teacher. I'm in this boring class about the Greek philosophers and playwrights. You have to know the mythology to understand the plays because they were always about the Greek gods. Very hard to keep up with all the names and relationships."

"Sounds more like people than gods."

"They were just as jealous and horny and vindictive. And sometimes really mean."

Ray's curiosity was piqued. She followed the girl to her classroom, and after everyone was seated, slipped into an empty chair at the back. She left the room enchanted.

She began sitting in on other classes as well. Except for the brief years she had partied with Mary, no one except Hans had ever noticed her. She had brown hair and eyes, pale skin, a somewhat neutral fashion sense, and was so slender she could disappear behind saplings. She was used to being ignored. She wasn't enrolled and wasn't earning college credits or paying for this opportunity to learn. And, as she didn't take tests or ask questions, her presence wasn't a burden to the instructors. So, she enjoyed a guilt-free theft of knowledge in classes large enough to hide her presence, always sitting in the back.

Her vocabulary grew along with her fascination for the Greeks, whose plays told their history, their politics, and their many gods' very human frailties. She went to the town's library where she read the mythology and the plays discussed in class.

Once again, man created not one but multiple gods in his own image.

Ray was most moved by an allegory written by Plato, an ancient Greek philosopher. It was the story of a man held in a cave. He sat in a row with other prisoners, chained, facing the back of the cave and unable to turn around or even look sideways. They only knew what they learned from the shadows on the cave wall created by the sunlight behind them. When someone walked past the entrance, their shadow on the wall was the prisoners' concept of reality.

One day the man was inexplicably released. He went out of the cave and, though it was difficult, learned to see in the bright light, learned to walk upright and to understand his new and wonderful world. He returned to the cave to release the others who had been in bondage with him. None of them would come. Although their knowledge was limited to shadows, they were afraid to leave what they knew. When he told them of the wonders of the world outside, they called him a liar, and had they not been chained, they would have killed him.

This story was written four hundred years before the birth

of Jesus, but the parallels were there. The man from the cave also would have been crucified by the very people he wished to enlighten.

The more times Ray read that story, the more she saw herself as a prisoner in a cave. But Allie was in the cave too, and Ray couldn't leave her any more than she could take her away. Allie wasn't ready to go, but her cave years would be temporary. When she was old enough and strong enough, she would find her way out, into the real world where pets and mothers did not simply disappear to a "better place."

Maybe I have been the one afraid of leaving. Maybe this town is my cave. Maybe I have imprisoned Allie in a misguided attempt to protect her.

Sometimes at night, after Allie was in bed, Ray went to the children's ward at the hospital where she whispered words of encouragement to the sleeping and told stories to those unable to sleep.

Ray believed the children who needed her most were those with cancer or other debilitating, chronic, and life-threatening disorders. They too were cave-dwellers, but not by choice. So, she made their cave a happy place. They sang and drummed with spoons and trays. Those who were able would march around the room. Eventually, a nurse would arrive and disrupt the fun with medications while Ray slipped away.

Because she was a sometime volunteer at the hospital and familiar to the nurses, they always tolerated her innocent interferences. They knew of her work at the hospice and welcomed the distractions she created for the children—within limits. The whole town seemed to see her as a strange but harmless oddity, living on the fringe of their society. She saw herself as a whiff of smoke.

Chapter Eighteen

Ray saw years as semesters, and the semesters passed. One Sunday in late September, Carla began a rare conversation while she sipped coffee in the kitchen and watched Ray wash the breakfast dishes.

"So, what keeps you busy all day?"

"I volunteer at the hospice…and other stuff." Ray carefully put a glass on a towel beside the sink.

"Yeah, about the 'other stuff.' A friend in AA tells me you've been taking classes over at the college."

"So what?"

"So, where did you get the money for that?"

Ray slammed a pot into the dish pan and violently scrubbed at the remains of burnt popcorn. "I'm just sitting in. I don't get credit. It doesn't cost anything."

"Apparently, it's not legal. She said I should warn you that someone would notice and make you stop."

"I've done it for nine semesters," Ray said, her voice tighter and louder. "If they've noticed, they don't care."

"If they've noticed and haven't stopped you, they must feel sorry for you. We may be poor, but we don't need charity!"

Ray put the last dish on the towel and turned to her mother with a defeated response. "All right. I won't go anymore." She went upstairs to dress.

When Ray returned from her waterfront church, she intercepted Ranny and Allie coming home from the Episcopal church. Ranny had dinner guests arriving soon, so Allie and Ray walked the rest of the way home without him, dawdling—looking at the last of summer's flowers or playing hopscotch without the need for a chalk-drawn pattern. They hopped and jumped, Allie led and Ray followed. She tried hard to turn the angry day into a happy one. Carla had gone to an AA meeting, so the house was empty. Ray went into the kitchen to fix lunch and Allie followed, chatting about her Sunday school lesson.

"It was about Jonah and the whale. Do you believe a man could be swallowed by a whale, live inside it, and then be thrown out—still alive?"

"I don't know. Maybe the story is a metaphor. People can be sort of swallowed up by their jobs, or by poverty, or lots of things that seem bigger than they are (like whales). It's kind of like being in a prison. If they have faith in themselves and maybe the goodness of others, they can be set free or escape. Does any of that make sense?"

"Yes. But my Sunday school teacher would say, 'if they have faith in God,' not in themselves or others."

"Probably. And the great thing is, Allie, you get to hear what others say (like your Sunday school teacher) and then decide what you think or believe."

"Yes, as you always remind me: I'm ten years old now—I can think for myself. But I don't think Jonah and the whale had anything to do with a prison break."

Ray laughed. "We'll talk about this again when you're twelve. Help me with lunch."

The next afternoon, when Ray came home after Carla had left but before Allie arrived from school, she found an envelope on the table with her name in Carla's loopy handwriting. She opened it to find cash and a note: "Enough for one class and maybe a secondhand textbook."

There had been money from the other driver's liability insurance after the crash. It had covered funeral expenses for Mary, medical expenses for Allie and Ray, and had allowed them to survive with the help of Carla's salary. Ray realized for the first time, as if stepping out of a fog, or a whale's belly, or a cave, that she needed a paying job. Allie was old enough to depend less on her.

She would take that class. She would allow some of the insurance money to make up for some of her loss. Ray laughed aloud, as she pictured herself in the front row of a classroom. She could ask questions, share opinions. She could choose smaller, more advanced classes…and earn college credit.

Ooooh! Dang! Guess I'll have to get my GED. On the other hand, that will make me the first Nichols woman to finish high school.

That one small act of kindness (or conscience) did not make up for the years of negativity between Carla and Ray, but it was a beginning, an interruption in the family's generations of failure to achieve a single educational degree.

Ray asked for a part-time paid position at the hospice center. Her schedule was set for school hours so she could be home in time to meet Allie, and was to include time for her to take one class per semester. The nurses spoke on her behalf, and it was agreed. Minimum wage was all she got and all she expected. She still managed to work thirty hours each week.

Ray had never been a consumer, but now she could afford to buy a few clothes and to introduce Allie to foods neither of them had ever tasted and a few minor luxuries Carla had not thought to provide. The rest was saved for her next college course and textbook.

Ray noticed a gradual change in Carla. She seemed more relaxed, complained less, and smiled more. She started giving Allie an allowance. Ray wondered if she had discovered a lost bag of money—or a man.

One day Ray and Allie came home to find a carpenter in their attic bedroom. He measured and took notes for the construction of a bathroom. To simplify plumbing, it was located directly above the bathroom on the second floor. Consequently, it was right in the middle of their room. It divided their space and provided a bit of privacy for each of them. Their own bathroom with toilet and tub was a luxury neither had ever hoped for—much less expected to come from Carla's tightly monitored income. Ray was convinced.

It must be a man. And he must be a sugar daddy.

Chapter Nineteen

Some girls lose their baby fat and begin their curves with the first flush of hormones. Not Allie. She continued to be short and plump through middle school with no promise of change, not in her body or her days of friendless routine.

In the eighth grade, the humdrum of Allie's life was altered forever. On a late spring day, she was sitting in algebra class, struggling with a problem on a quiz. She tapped her pencil on her desk. It helped her think. The answer didn't come, so she tapped harder. She found a pattern and a rhythm. Behind her, she heard more taps, enhancing her own. For a moment, she thought it was Ray—sounded like her—but it couldn't be, not in her classroom. At the front desk, Mrs. Reynolds absently tapped her toe and drummed with her fingers. Irritated students looked up from their papers and craned their necks to find the disruptive sounds.

Mrs. Reynolds abruptly stopped; Allie's pencil paused in midair; but the sound behind her built to a crescendo and a dramatic ending. The teacher cleared her throat, demanding silence. All heads slowly swiveled back to stare at their papers.

At the end of class, Allie stole a look behind her. The boy with long hair and a toothy grin said, "Hey! My name's Bernie. We've never met. That was really cool."

Mrs. Reynolds interrupted, prevented Allie from slinking out without a response.

"Bernie, you're dismissed. Allie," she continued after Bernie left, "have you ever had lessons?"

"In what?"

"In drumming, of course."

"Uh, no ma'am. I'm…I'm sorry that I disturbed the class."

"I suspect the distraction was welcome…When I was in high school, I played trumpet in the marching band. I think Bernie plays drums in a garage band. You should get lessons this summer and audition next year. Band turned high school hell into a joy for me."

"Uh, okay," Allie responded. But she knew there would be no money for drums or lessons.

"And I know someone who might loan you their son's drums for the summer. He lost interest a long time ago."

When Allie finally broke away, she found Bernie in the hall. It was the last class of the day, and he walked her home. The tall skinny boy and the short plump girl seemed not to fit, but it was the beginning of an unending friendship.

Allie told Ray about the incident and was encouraged to ask Carla for lessons. To their mutual surprise, she agreed without hesitation. After Allie ran upstairs to do her homework, Ray looked at her mother.

"What?" Ray asked, confused by the turning of the we-can't-afford-it screw.

"Not to be denied!" Carla replied with her secret smile, and then left for her evening shift.

Ray threw herself into a chair, happy for Allie, but unable to suppress a niggling anger at Carla.

I wonder if the new bathroom would have been built if Allie slept on the second floor instead of with me in the attic...not to be denied...what the hell?

Chapter Twenty

All summer long, from the moment Carla left the house until she returned, Allie played her drums in the attic. It was a magical time. She had weekly lessons, learning the basic drumming techniques and how to read music, but every afternoon she went to Bernie's house and he released her to play what was in her soul—not the notes on paper.

When school began, they both signed up for marching band. Allie had difficulty playing the music and executing drill moves at the same time. She could remember the notes and the moves, but she couldn't maintain the imposed beat. Her hands and feet always wanted to improvise. It was just as bad for Bernie, but his problem was a lack of coordination. They spent every evening after everyone else left, going over the movements.

Ray often sat in the bleachers and watched.

But even Allie didn't realize that she had been inside herself for so long, ignoring and ignored by everyone else, that she didn't know how to be part of a group—like the marching band.

"So why did they let you in the band?" Ray asked one evening after Allie complained about her own inept marching.

"You ask me that whenever I get discouraged."

"And the answer is?"

"Because I can out-drum every other kid in the state—maybe the world."

"That's my girl—my drummer girl."

The first home game was on a beautiful September evening. At halftime, the sun had just begun to set. Allie's band marched onto the field. The instruments flashed in the stadium lights as the marchers turned in intricate movements. Everything was fine until the drumline began its solo. Allie and Bernie were both able to play all the drums and other percussion instruments, but they had been assigned to play large bass drums.

In spite of their usual missteps, they both did well until the line marched away from the stands, stopped, turned, then turned again, and faced the bleachers where Ray sat, unable to breathe. Allie was in front, marching in place. When it was time to move, she didn't...Bernie had stepped on her pant leg.

Dammit! I meant to shorten those pants.

Ray saw a look of panic on Allie's face, and knew she had lost it—the beat, the choreography, everything. She just stopped. Bernie ran into her, and the rest of the drumline ran into him, pushing Allie forward. Separated from the others, she began to turn and then spin. Her drum flashed in the stadium lights like a giant bedazzled marshmallow.

Everyone in the bleachers was silent. The whole field of marchers had stopped moving and playing. Then Allie stopped, frozen by the silence. Ray saw her eyes lose focus, saw her hands begin to drum a new beat. Bernie joined her as he had done long ago in their math class. One at a time, the other drummers found the new beat.

Ray kept praying, *don't dance!* But she did. When the drumming reached its peak of volume, the crowd stood up and cheered for the drummer girl. Ray laughed with relief at the stunned but delightfully surprised spectators.

Allie, however, was mortified.

When the crowd's applause made her pause, the drum major saw his chance and signaled the brass. They all picked up where they were supposed to at the end of the drumline solo. The sound snapped Allie back to reality, and she began marching in place again—but well away from Bernie's feet. The rest of it was a blur for her and for Ray, who listened with pride to the awed comments from the crowd of parents and students.

When they exited the field, two boys from the drumline jumped on her, but Bernie pulled them off. The rest of the band thought they had practiced the new moves in secret. Some were angry; some were impressed; no one knew what to expect from Mr. Sam, the band director.

The following Monday, Allie could not meet Mr. Sam's eyes, but he held her back after class, much like her math teacher had done the year before. And, like her, he didn't scold but talked to her about her unique music and said he had decided to put it into the drumline routine—but without the spinning and dancing. He started a jazz band in the spring, and Allie found a new passion.

Chapter Twenty-One

Allie and Bernie continued to be closer than friends, but always as a part of their group, never quite ready to date or try anything more intimate—not even a kiss. At graduation, Ray photographed them as they hugged. Allie had grown a few inches in high school, and Bernie didn't have to bend so far down to hold her. It was a long hug, and Ray believed they had silently said goodbye.

Bernie went west to Colorado to study architecture, and thanks to an unexpected full-ride scholarship, Allie went north, to an Ivy League school. Ray knew it was time for her to be on her own, but also felt the hollow where her heart should be when they hugged and cried their goodbyes.

Her own classes did not lead to the completion of a specific major. Because her interests were so varied, and she had not received credit for the classes she had illegally sat in on, she felt undirected, unable to break her life's fragmented pattern.

Ray wondered why she stayed, why she didn't move on—or at least forward. She signed up for a psychology class and then tried to analyze herself. There were some amusing conversations as she looked in the mirror and asked herself questions about her childhood and her relationship with her mother...and Hans. Her reflection in the mirror became more interesting whenever she tried to skirt the truth.

Still she pondered Plato's story of the cave, and Ray gradually began to see it not as a place but rather a state of mind. It was about the various attitudes and -*isms* ingrained in people: racism, sexism, and all the other -*isms* at the root of most social and ethical problems. She laughed when she learned that Plato didn't especially like the arts, thought they carried too much power. For him, the cave was a place of ignorance, and the outside world was a source of knowledge. She wondered if he rolled in his grave, knowing his allegory had lived for thousands of years as a piece of art as well as philosophy.

Chapter Twenty-Two

Allie went to her roommate's home in Maine for fall break while eastern North Carolina endured hurricane Isabel.

Carla stayed with a friend in a brick apartment building where she felt more secure. Raynelle refused to leave and hunkered down in their ancient wood-frame home to meet the hurricane on her own.

Isabel was a fierce storm that sounded and felt to Ray like a train passing over the house. A pine tree snapped in half and came through a kitchen window. Then power was lost. Awed by the force of nature and the resilience of her cave, she watched the shadows on the living room wall created by flickering candlelight. In the morning Isabel was gone, and Ray rolled off the couch into several inches of water.

She wandered the early dawn streets, stunned by the damage but heartened by the people as they stepped carefully through the debris, began their cleanup, and helped one another.

Allie's tree with the swing was damaged but not destroyed. Their metal shingles had weathered many storms and survived this one as well. But with downed limbs, trash in the yard and some loosened siding, the house looked like it had been in a brawl. In truth it only had a black eye or two and water damage from rain that blew through the broken window and seeped under the doors from flooded streets. As the locals would say, "The house has good bones." It still stood, battered and proud. Best of all, it qualified for help from FEMA. In a short time, the water had drained out and Carla returned to help Ray shovel sludge and throw out ruined furniture.

A group of men from a black church just a block away went to houses in the neighborhood and helped with temporary repairs. They replaced or nailed coverings over missing or shattered windows, reattached and caulked loose boards, and covered roof damage with tarps or plywood until professionals could finish the work. They also repaired porch steps and railings that could cause accidents, especially for the elderly. In the past, Ray had seen them build wheelchair ramps, mostly for their own church members. The storm seemed to erase racial and religious lines.

A few days after Isabel, they came to Carla's bruised house and offered to cover the broken window.

"I have a new window on the back porch." And with no shame or hesitation, she added, "Would you install it for me?"

A middle-aged balding man stepped forward.

"Link, stay with me. The rest of you can go on to the next house."

He introduced himself as Abraham Wright and his grown son as Link. Ray suspected (and was correct) that Link was short for Lincoln.

As Ray came to know these two men, she thought Abraham and his son had as much of a presidential look as any candidate in the last election, probably more—although Lincoln's buddies called him The Missing Link.

There had been only two men in Carla's life: her father and Ray's father. Either one of them would have frightened a woman into a lesbian relationship. But in spite of everything, Carla's blood still ran hot and heterosexual. Ray could almost see it course through her veins as she shook hands with Abraham Wright and began a conversation that would continue.

It seemed they already knew each other. Carla knew Abe from one of her AA groups. Because of personal contributions in meetings, they were already intimately acquainted.

Against her sponsor's advice, Carla saw more and more of the handsome black widower. She took a lot of teasing from the other AA women about meeting Mr. Right. She also ignored a lot of racist reactions. Ray was begrudgingly and surprisingly proud of her.

As they saw more of each other, Ray saw less. She avoided the house, where they were discovering and exploring their new-found love. Instead, she haunted the hospital and hospice at all hours of the day and night.

Christmas without Allie loomed in the near future. But Ray chose to stay home while Carla and Abe went to Boston. She rationalized there were patients and neighbors who needed her more during their lonely holidays, many still recovering from Isabel.

Chapter Twenty-Three

Ray had not driven since before the crash. A kind of panic took over whenever she got into a car, much less sat in the driver's seat. Will finally replaced his fifteen-year-old Subaru with a new one and offered the keys of his old but well-maintained car to Ray.

"Merry Christmas," he smiled.

Ray walked most places, but she couldn't get from the hospice to the college without risking being late for class. The hospice van that was used to transport patients had often provided her with a ride, but the availability was unpredictable. So, she reluctantly accepted the gift that seemed too generous but afforded a solution.

"It wouldn't bring much as a trade-in…And, more importantly, I think it's time you conquered your fear of driving." He asked her for a dollar and transferred the title to her name, then drove her for insurance and to get a new driver's license. Her original one had never been renewed.

"I'm thirty-two," she whispered, almost embarrassed. "Why do I feel like I'm sixteen?"

"You've been in limbo for half your life, Ray. Maybe it's time to move forward."

She agreed, but refused to drive home. "Let me do this in my own time. Today has already had enough challenges."

In return for the amazing gift, Ray made mounds of Christmas candy for Will to share with their many holiday guests. Ranny took a tin of it to the Emporium each day,

"I didn't plan for the candy to be a bribe," he reported to Ray, "but every time someone takes a piece, I think they feel obligated to buy something. Can I pay you to make more?"

"You can buy the ingredients," she laughed.

With the college closed for the holidays, and no need to drive the car, Ray simply sat in it for hours, trying to control her nerves and the images that exploded in her mind: the old

Mustang crumpled like a handful of aluminum foil, Mary upside-down and unconscious, Allie's screams.

One day she forced herself to turn on the ignition. Then she put it in drive and slowly steered the car to the Pamlico River. She looked at the sailboats and motorboats large enough to sleep four or more and to navigate the Intracoastal Waterway down to Florida or up to New England. In the midst of her daydreams, she was surprised to see Eric Masters sitting on a bench.

She parked, got out, and walked to the bench where she sat beside him. She wondered if he remembered her. She should have known better. Of course he did. He was the man who fell asleep at the wheel and changed the destiny of all she held dear. How could he forget any of them? He said nothing, just stared at the gently rocking boats.

"I forgave you long ago, Mr. Masters," Ray whispered.

"Can you really forgive me for taking a mother away from a child, for destroying so many lives?"

"You're right. It isn't my forgiveness that matters. It's time you forgave yourself."

"Easy to say," he sighed. "And, how are you?"

"It's probably time for both of us to move on…You know it wasn't entirely your fault." His eyebrows lifted in question. "We were a wreck just waiting to happen."

"Thank you," he breathed, then rose and walked away.

And who am I to talk about forgiving yourself? And what made me conjure that poor dead man into my own guilt and reality?

She got back in the car and drove all over town, smiling in celebration of this newfound freedom and control over fear and time.

Chapter Twenty-Four

Allie came home that spring, arriving in the used Jeep Carla had bought her. She ran into the house and up the attic stairs in search of her cousin. Ray held up both hands in the "stop!" position and stared at the young woman before her. There was no plump little girl and no glasses.

"Contacts? And, how did you grow so tall and so slim so fast?"

Allie laughed. "Yes, contacts and heels, but I did grow two inches taller. My roommates bullied me into a makeover." When Rays eyes narrowed into a frown, Allie added, "I guess it was soft-core bullying, and I didn't fight back. They put me on a diet from the first week I was there. I thought I would starve to death. They said I would attract the wrong kind of guy."

"That's cruel!"

Allie shrugged, and Ray finally pulled her into a hug.

"And stupid!" Allie added. "Their good-looking rich guys weren't nearly as much fun as Bernie and our gang of misfits."

She spun away, letting Ray see again how she had lost the baby fat and found her curves. "But I did let them remake me. Guess I wondered how the other half lived—the cool half."

"And what did you learn?"

She stopped spinning and fell onto her bed. "That I missed Bernie...that I was uncomfortable in someone else's skin. That I was still a misfit, and just pretending to be cool...still painfully shy...didn't really want to be one of them."

"Did you write to him?" Ray dropped into a chair while Allie rose, opened her suitcase, and began emptying it.

"We emailed, daily at first. Then we both got busy. Anyway, I had a boyfriend, but it didn't last."

"I predict there will be others." Ray said, in a gypsy-weirdo voice and then watched in shock as Allie began hanging up her unpacked clothes.

Who is this imposter? Where's my messy girl?

"When the guys found out that I was still a virgin and wouldn't go down on anyone who invited me to his frat house or bought me a hamburger, I stopped getting dates."

"Whoa…words, girl…and images."

"Sorry, Raynelle. You look like a college girl. And that's all I've been around lately— except for professors."

"It's okay." Ray looked down at her own attire—t-shirt and cutoffs—and agreed that she did not look like an adult. "I guess when you live on campus, it can be an insulated world."

"Even though there are twenty thousand students, from all over the country—from all over the world—there's a sameness on some levels…mainly the dating level." She stopped hanging clothes and sat on the bed. She looked directly into Ray's eyes. "Were you a virgin at my age, Raynelle?"

Ray laughed, pulling her knees up, circling legs with arms. "Your mother and I were pretty wild those last years before the crash. So, I guess the answer is no, I wasn't a virgin at your age. I don't remember much about it—the sex—except that it was meaningless, without feeling. When I finally lost all interest and began refusing their demands, I was told that I must be frigid or a lesbian."

Ray couldn't speak her real thought. *I wanted to be with Hans Nielson, and always fantasized it was him on top of me. But it wasn't him and the fantasy always ended in disappointment.*

"Men can be jerks! But that's exactly how I feel. Kissing is great, and touching. But I want sex to be something more than just satisfying curiosity or doing what's expected—sometimes demanded."

"It will happen—when you're ready." Ray hesitated for a moment, and then made a decision. "The truth is I had a pregnancy scare, a late period. It made me realize that I was tempting fate, risking making the same mistake Carla and Mary made."

Allie looked up with surprised eyes. "Were we mistakes, Ray?"

"No, of course not, but that's how our mothers saw us. I'm not saying you should avoid sex out of fear. Just be careful." She didn't say there was someone whose love would have made her risk everything.

"Are you seeing anyone now?" Allie asked.

"No, not since the crash." Allie's survival and well-being had been Ray's only focus for so many years—even though she was clearly no longer a needy child.

"Maybe it's time, Miss Raynelle."

"Maybe it's not your business, Miss Alabama."

The next day Bernie arrived home for his summer break and called. Allie's wait ended.

When he picked her up that night for their first real date, Ray was again taken back by change. He was over six feet tall, but less gangly than before. His long hair had been cut in that short, messy fashion that makes grown men look like playful boys, makes them approachable, huggable. But it was his face that caught Ray. It wasn't handsome in the traditional way; his features weren't perfect, but they hinted at what they would become: strong, full of character, and very sexy. His eyes roamed over Allie, and Ray hoped he really saw her—not the pretty girl in tight jeans and a tank top that showed the rest of her curves, not the woman she had morphed into—but the smart, talented, perfect individual she had always been.

Of course, she was kidding herself. He saw the brand-new Allie.

An energy passed between them and actually lit up the room. They didn't speak. They didn't touch. They just left.

Carla and Abe had been vacationing in Jamaica, soon to move on to Trinidad. The old house had finally become Ray's when Carla moved into Abe's river place the previous month. But Ray wandered the streets that night, not sure she wanted to be home when Allie and Bernie came back. Maybe it was the frustration of wanting to protect her and being unable to. Maybe it was jealousy. Allie would make her own decisions with or without the presence of her self-appointed guardian. She rationalized that she was being kind, respecting their choices and their privacy.

Nah! It's jealousy.

Chapter Twenty-Five

Returning the next morning, Ray found Allie in the kitchen, wearing sleeping shorts and a big t-shirt. She was quiet as she poached an egg and brewed coffee.

"When did you learn to fend for yourself?" Ray asked and sat at the table, still awed by Allie's slender beauty and the way her eyes (once a distraction) were now her greatest asset.

"When I no longer had you to fend for me. I can't cook as well as you, but my roommates taught me a few simple things we could make with a hotplate, a microwave, or a toaster oven. And I remembered how you make salad dressings and gravy without a recipe. Actually, I learned a lot from you. The cafeteria food at college is unhealthy, with too much salt and sugar. Mostly my roommates and I graze on raw vegetables."

"You have a refrigerator in your dorm room? And they let you use a hot plate?"

She laughed. "Everyone has a fridge and a microwave, and we hide the hot plate when we're not using it. You should come see it—the campus and my room…and Boston."

"Yes, Boston. I knew someone who moved there years ago. Anyway, I would like to visit, but I feel geographically bound to this town. Besides, you wisely didn't want me following you to college."

"I missed you—almost came home a dozen times. But I knew inside that I had to stick it out, had to finish the year… had to do it on my own." She sat with her plate and ate, avoiding Ray's eyes. "I was afraid you wouldn't be here when I came back. I think that's why I didn't come home during the holidays or breaks." Her voice faded with what was a kind of apology and admission.

Allie's smile changed the mood. "By the way, I love the new kitchen and all the other improvements. Hooray for FEMA— and for Abe! I'm sure he augmented the insurance and the government's contribution to raise the house and bring it up to code.

And I love the exterior paint. What's it called?"

"The paint store calls it Sonoma Sunset. Ranny calls it Ashes of Roses—makes me feel like Delta Dawn, the woman in the country song. You should phone Ranny and Will, let them know you're home. And Carla probably paid for the improvements that FEMA didn't cover. You know how proud she is. Your scholarship saved her a lot of the money she'd been putting aside for years.

Allie ate while Ray hummed the refrain from "Delta Dawn." Finished, she stared at her plate before looking up. "Why *are* you still here, Ray?"

"I'm not ready to leave yet. You're taller, but you're not grown."

"Are you saying I'll get even taller?"

"No, but I'm afraid you've grown faster than I expected in other ways, sweet girl. Now what's that phrase I always hear young people use? Oh yeah, something about an elephant in the room?"

Allie rose and poured herself another cup of coffee as a small smile began on her lips. "You mean, Bernie—and last night."

"No details, please. I just want to know, out of curiosity… was it all you expected?"

She hesitated before responding, looking anywhere but at Ray. "It was awkward but not, wonderful but frightening, and otherwise amazing—the feel of skin on skin…" She stopped, blushing.

Skin on skin.

The words evoked feelings and images, starting a warmth that began at Ray's face and ended at her toes.

"But I'm confused, Ray, not sure what to think. Bernie and I have been friends forever. We know almost everything about each other. In some ways, it would have been easier with a stranger. At the same time, it was perfect." She covered her face with her hands and groaned at her own contradictions.

"So, what's wrong then?"

"I'm just not sure we're ready for this—with school and so much distance. You know, I could never talk like this to my roommates—in fact, I hardly ever really talk to them. We have nothing in common except sharing rooms. You and Bernie are the only people I've ever been able to be open and natural with. You're the only people who get me."

"Do you love him, Allie?"

"I don't know. I do love being with him. I miss him when we're apart. Is that love?"

Ray wished she could provide the answer. "Do you need to make that decision now?"

"He wants me to transfer to Colorado. But they don't have the music program I need. And my scholarship wouldn't transfer."

"Is music more important than Bernie?"

"I don't know." She looked miserable. "I need music in my life, and not just as a hobby. And whatever I do, I want to do well—better than well."

"Allie, Bernie has been a big part of your growing up. He matters. Your music is a part of who you are. It matters. But most of all, you matter."

"To you, maybe."

"No, sweetheart—to everyone you touch. But remember this: if you aren't happy, you can't make him happy. And to further confuse the issue, time is your friend and your enemy. Use it wisely, but use it."

Ray would have said, "What's another three years?" But she knew that at Allie's age, a three-year wait would seem like an eternity.

Chapter Twenty-Six

"What's the story on the Harmon house?" Allie asked the following day. "I noticed the 'For Sale' sign is gone. A man I've never seen sits on the porch in a rocking chair."

Ray closed the book she had been reading. "Yes. Not a good story. They moved in two months ago. The house looks so pretty on the outside, but as you know, the Harmons only renovated the first floor and, with our real estate market in a slump, it didn't sell until they reduced the price to match the economy."

"Boston's economy seems fine."

"No surprise. But small towns are slower to recover from a recession."

"What's their story—the new owners?"

"They have a son—eight or nine. The father sits on the porch from early morning till dark—just goes inside for meals and to sleep. His wife sits with him much of the time. Carla got a letter when they moved in that exposed our new neighbor, Frank Darby, to be a registered sex offender."

"Whoa! Man! Have you met them?"

"Will told me he isn't receptive to visitors. He suggested we respect Mr. Darby's need for privacy, give him time to adjust. He was in prison for two years."

"Whoa, a sex offender! What about the boy? I mean, is he safe?"

"At home, yes," Ray huffed. "But, maybe because of his dad's history, he's a target for other kids—especially bullies. His name is Marcus. He's a bit of a misfit, like you and I were."

"You mean he hears a different drummer?"

"Several."

As weeks passed, the Darbys continued their isolation, except for Marcus, who would walk to the river or downtown, usually carrying a stick. Ray wondered if it was a weapon meant to keep taunting kids at bay. Whenever she encountered him near the marina, he turned around and took a different route home.

Ray's curiosity about Frank Darby's real story grew, becoming a need to know—a need stronger than her respect for his wish for privacy. After all, in this world of easy access to digital technology, there was little chance of privacy for anyone, anyway.

She went to Allie's computer and did an in-depth search on Frank Darby. She found his story in various news articles rather than just the website for sexual predators.

When he was only twenty-five, Frank went to a bachelor party for a friend. He drank too much and, after some girls joined the party, he was awakened from a state of unconsciousness by the police.

The party was busted and everyone arrested. Frank was convicted of rape of a fourteen-year-old. After two years in prison, the high school prostitution ring that had solicited the girl was broken. Being underaged, she was also considered a victim—even if she might have been willing. No longer afraid of repercussions, she confessed there had been no sexual act between them. Frank was released—his conviction reversed. But, because he'd been found with a naked and underage girl, he'd been unable to expunge the record of his arrest as a sexual predator.

Someone should have talked to that judge! The man was unconscious!

Ray didn't know what Frank must have experienced in prison and didn't want to guess. But she thought it might explain his desire to stay apart—and to remain outside on his porch, after all that time in a cage.

The girl's wealthy family had known the truth and had lied for her, letting Frank go to prison in order to protect her. His lawyer successfully sued them in civil court and won an income for Frank's family. After all, he could no longer work at his profession—a middle school guidance counselor. And few people are willing to hire sex offenders for any job.

Chapter Twenty-Seven

Allie and Bernie both worked summer jobs but spent evenings and weekends together. He continued to press her to transfer to Colorado but seemed to never entertain the thought of moving east, to her campus and life.

Near the end of July, Ray could see Allie letting go, backing away from Bernie. By the first week of August, they were arguing, finding fault, but more importantly—finding ways to justify their decisions to continue their educations in separate schools. Bernie left first. After three days of crying, Allie returned to Boston.

For the following summer breaks, Bernie had apprenticeships in various locations, and Allie came home to Ray, their attic music room, and their river.

Following graduation, Allie was planning on a gap year to travel and reconnect with Bernie. And then graduate school—wherever he found employment. Bernie, who had never stopped playing the drums, set aside his architectural degree when he was recruited into the Marines.

"You what?" she whispered into the phone.

"I'm on my way to boot camp. I'm sorry. I just couldn't talk about it until I knew for certain. It's the Marine Band, Allie. Architecture can wait. You know I only did that for my parents, anyway. My heart has always been in music. I'll get to perform, travel, develop my drumming skills...maybe even make a career of it."

After a long silence, she mumbled, "I'm happy for you," and hung up the phone.

Her year of travel suddenly became an exercise in loneliness.

Allie's high school band director, Sam Partridge, was offered a last-minute contract to teach and direct at a small, well-respected college in West Virginia. He encouraged Allie to apply for his vacated position. She did, without hesitation.

Her application was well-received, but Carla learned from

the principal's husband (a member of AA) that his wife was reluctant to hire someone who carried a reputation of being different, maybe even crazy. Carla assured him that Allie had never been crazy, but admittedly had been different. A letter of support from Mr. Sam and her major professor in Boston tipped the scales, and Allie was hired.

Principal Whiting called her in to sign her contract. "This is conditional, Ms. Nichols. First, the band has to continue a comparable level of success in competitions it experienced under Sam Partridge, and second, you must fulfill the role of a respected faculty member with no question regarding your mental stability."

The conditions and the attitude gave her pause, but Allie acquiesced. She had been so hurt and depressed since Bernie's phone call, she wasn't convinced of the truth of her own response. "I'm not unstable, Principal Whiting. You can depend on me to be a conscientious teacher and band director."

Instead of feeling confident with her new crisp diploma in hand, she felt lost—as if she belonged nowhere. Ray, however, provided safety and love.

At Bernie's urging, she decided she would stay for two years while she searched for the perfect next position in or near Washington, D.C., where the Marine band was based.

She spent the summer creating lesson plans for the classes she would teach, inventorying the equipment and instruments, and planning the theme and music for the marching band competitions.

"Oh my God, Ray," she moaned after the first week of classes. "I am overwhelmed. Student teaching did not prepare me for this. Nothing could prepare me for this."

"How can I help?" Ray chirped.

"Stop being so damned cheerful! Most of the band graduated last year. I'm having to build something out of nothing. And they have no discipline—and no respect for me."

"So, you need to get their attention. Use your drumstick."

"What? I'm not allowed to hit them."

"Think about it."

And she did.

The next day when her students came to the band room, talking and laughing, they found Allie at her desk with a microphone and a drumstick. She began tapping on the desk, much like when she had tapped with her pencil during a math exam so many years before. The microphone magnified the sound and the students gradually stopped their talking and sat in the arranged chairs.

Allie paused and said, "Join me. Find the beat and use whatever you have—your hands, your feet, a pencil, or whatever you can find to make a percussion sound. See if you can keep up." She began slowly, initiating a simple beat and then gradually making it more complex. The students focused and followed, slapping their thighs, stomping their feet, or clapping their hands. The percussionists found sticks and tapped on the chair-back in front of them or on the floor.

Then Allie picked up another drumstick and slid over to the drums she had set up beside her desk and began to demonstrate real drumming. The class stopped their own sounds, unable to keep up and just listened and stared while she performed for them. When she finished, they applauded.

She held up her drumstick for quiet. "Are you here to screw around...or are you here to make music?"

Their readiness to follow her was demonstrated by their instant stomping, clapping, and cheering.

The marching band was good but not as successful in competitions as it had been under Mr. Sam. However, they usually placed in the top four, and always received high ratings for creativity. They were young with a new director still learning her way.

The only kink in Allie's contentment with her new life as a teacher was the behavior of the bullies who targeted band members. Reminded of her own public-school days, she too felt intimidated. She isolated herself in the band room, too busy to join the general school population except when she had lunch duty or faculty meetings that required her attendance. So, she was surprised when she did step out of her space to see shy smiles from students that suggested respect—even awe.

The awe was inspired by the annual event that won everyone's praise and bolstered Allie's confidence, the spring jazz concert. It only took one season for everyone to know where her real talent resided.

Ray hadn't seen Allie's skills evolve while she was away in college, but when her students rehearsed their first jazz concert she was there and saw a different Allie emerge.

She put her drumstick down and lifted her hand, silently calling for their attention. She snapped her fingers once, twice, and two more times—initiating the beat. With the first notes she began moving, almost imperceptibly, from her head down to her feet, every part of her body communicating the music.

Stiff and self-conscious at first, her students gradually let her lead them into the same immersion, living and breathing the music. Some rose from their seats, almost dancing while they played. When they were completely loose and out of control, she quieted them by tapping the music stand with her stick.

"All right. You have the idea. Let's do it again. This time, don't show off. Don't think about your movements; don't force them; don't try to be cool; think only about the music. Stay relaxed but engaged, and the physical response will be there. Oh, and don't stand up unless you have a solo."

Her jazz band grew to be the entertainment focus of the county. Ray was always there, listening and watching—not only the performance, but also the audience. She knew for a fact that many of the men came to see Allie, who had no idea how mesmerizing she became when the music filled her. The same intensity of feeling was reflected in each member of the band, and it always brought the audience ultimately to its feet.

No wonder the school bullies hate her—and hate her students, Ray thought. *They share something magical, something that can't be touched by any amount of taunting abuse and can't be diminished or taken away.*

In spite of or with the help of her successes, Allie began her search for a teaching position in or near Washington, D.C. She soon had two schools in the area with openings, one of them a private school for the arts. She updated her resume and sent it with videos of the marching band and jazz band.

Chapter Twenty-Eight

Time passed quickly the first two years of teaching as Allie struggled to develop her marching band and fulfill all the performance and teaching responsibilities. Bernie did not come home, but encouraged his parents and Allie to visit where he was performing. He no longer texted except in response to questions from Allie. Instead of sharing the events in his life, he seemed to be increasingly more preoccupied. She wondered if she seemed the same to him. They were both, after all, beginning their careers and were both very busy.

She scheduled an appointment for an interview at the private school in Alexandria and texted Bernie that she would be at his performance in Philadelphia.

She left early in the morning of a Friday teacher workday and drove to Virginia for an afternoon interview. She returned the next morning, eyes red and swollen from crying for the last seven hours of driving from Philadelphia after the Marine Band concert.

"I take it you didn't get the job?" Ray asked, sympathetic but also relieved and hopeful.

Allie held a cold wet washcloth to her eyes and sighed. "I think I waited too long. I could hear in his voice on the phone and even in his texts and emails that Bernie was more and more happy with the life he has without me than with one that might include me."

"Why don't you tell me what happened. Start with the interview."

"All right," she sighed, leaning back on the couch. "It's a beautiful campus. You could imagine that if a leaf fell from a tree, there would be someone there to scoop it up before anyone saw."

"This is a high school, right?"

"Yes, but while I waited for my interview, I saw a catalog for the school. The faculty and administrative staff listed in the front looked more like it belonged to a university. I was stunned by the number of MAs, MFAs, or PhDs after almost all the names. I was also stunned to see there was a large music program with a five-person faculty.

"I realized that my interview was a huge mistake. But before I could make an excuse and escape, I was called into a conference room."

At this point Allie sat up and removed the washcloth from her face. She began an exaggerated imitation of the pompous interviewer.

"He introduced himself as Brian Halston, chair of the search committee to replace their band director, who is also chair of the music department, retiring next spring—PhD. Next, he informed me that I was not even being considered."

"Without even interviewing you?"

"He gestured to a seat, and then looked through a window at his educational domain. When I tried to speak, he turned and stopped me.

"He said, and I quote, 'We, the committee, agreed to this interview because we were impressed by the video of your jazz concert. We understand this is your first teaching position, but you have achieved a lot in a relatively short time. We are looking for someone with more experience and, of course, a graduate degree for the position of chair. You are, however, on our short list to replace the director of our jazz band.'"

"Is he or she leaving?" Ray inserted, laughing at Allie's imitation of Halston's lofty speech and mannerisms.

"'Not by choice,' he said, 'but as the current jazz band director has not pursued a graduate degree, the position may be available by next fall. In the meantime, you might register for some graduate courses. You can get them online if there isn't a nearby university with a graduate program.'"

"A graduate online degree in what?" Ray asked with disbelief that any music degree could be achieved online.

"Music education, or music history, or something

else—math, English. In other words, they don't care what the degree is in as long as it puts initials behind your name in their catalog. He then crossed to the door and opened it wide, obviously waiting for me to collect my unopened portfolio, purse, and barely opened mouth. 'We will stay in touch,' he added as I left."

"Would you do that?" Ray asked. "I mean start an online graduate program?"

"I don't have time for all I need to do for my classes and the band performances now. I can't imagine complicating my life more than it already is. There's not even any assurance that I would get the job."

"Okay!" Ray said, wanting to get to the real problem. "Now, how was the concert?"

Allie looked down at her hands and put the washcloth on the side table, apparently through with tears, and resigned. She spoke calmly and softly.

"Bernie's performance last night was at a large auditorium in Philadelphia. Once again, as I read the program, I was impressed by the experience and degrees held, this time not by the director but by the performers. Many, like Bernie, held professional degrees in unrelated fields, but had chosen the Marines and music as their careers. I have to admit that I was moved by my own feeling of patriotism and the palpable love and pride of country their music inspired in the entire audience."

"Sounds like the band might be tough competition for his affection."

"Even for his attention...I went with Bernie and two of his band-brother Marines to a nearby restaurant after the performance. The talk was of the music and was interrupted many times by people who had been in the audience and wanted to congratulate them on their show or to get an autograph."

His Marine buddies were clearly used to the admiration of others, and the attention of young women. But they had still whistled appreciatively when they first saw pretty Allie beside Bernie.

"There was no discussion of my interview or our future. No time for a personal conversation. I had hoped we would have privacy later—even the night together. But he said they had to get back to the bus. There was another performance, a matinee, scheduled in another town today."

"And I'll bet you were hoping for the weekend," Ray sighed, beginning to understand Allie's grief and tears. It wasn't the interview. That she would laugh off as a lesson learned.

"Oh, he has the rest of the weekend off," she huffed, "but he's going upstate for skiing with the guys from our table. When I didn't say anything, he had the grace to add, 'Been planned a long time. John's family's expecting us.' John and the other guy both looked uncomfortable that Bernie clearly hadn't shared anything about their plans but had let me drive all that way for just a performance and quick dinner."

"I'm so sorry, Allie."

"So, I left the restaurant at almost midnight and drove all the way home...I wouldn't have been able to sleep anyway. And...at least I had time to reconsider the immediate future. I don't think a snooty private school with a pumped-up catalog is for me...For now, I'm happy to be here."

Chapter Twenty-Nine

It was the end of the school day the following fall. Allie walked around the main building to the band room. She heard sounds of anger coming from her left, behind the back door of the cafeteria, which was blocked from view by a concrete wall. Like any responsible teacher, she followed the sounds and was momentarily struck dumb by what she saw.

Five boys had formed a semicircle and backed another against a dumpster with overflowing trash. One broke from the ring and sauntered toward the smaller boy, while the others laughed with false bravado. Their victim, red with fearless fury, pulled a knife. Allie recognized him. He worked in the cafeteria, and he lived across the street from her—the Darby boy.

The other boys reacted in shock to the weapon, backing up a step. The one who had been approaching their victim howled in mock fear and dropped to his knees, raising his arms in exaggerated surrender. A clown.

"All right, this is over. Drop the knife!" she commanded, moving toward them with more determination than courage.

"No!" Marcus Darby responded, his eyes never leaving the boy opposite him who now rose to his full height and towered.

She knew the bullies were probably more bluster than bite and wouldn't get near that blade. She was more concerned about the boy with the knife being expelled because he'd brought a weapon to school. Principal Whiting would not compromise.

She paused for only a moment, and then moved in front of the forward aggressor and stood between him and Marcus. She turned, her back to the knife, only inches away from the leader of the bullies, and looked up into his face.

"I know every one of you," she lied as she struggled for calm. "Get...out!" There are times when clarity of purpose replaces fear and even common sense.

Two of the boys, clearly twins, sweated and shifted their eyes away. Tall and thin, they had the decency to seem ashamed.

Another, even taller and overweight, tried to intimidate her with his bold stares. He too was nervous, although he tried to sound cool.

"Slammin' body! How they pay attention in class with her walkin' around?" He laughed, but no one joined him.

The fourth was small, a redhead, and seemed not to fit in with this bunch that used size to intimidate.

And last, the boy who had dared to approach Marcus and his knife—a different story. She did know his name. It was Buck Bailey.

Allie had heard about Buck—new student, already gaining followers and a bad rep. He scared her. But she looked into his eyes without flinching.

"I said, "Get...out...now!"

Buck returned her look with a smile and a cool expression that clearly implied, *"Another time; this isn't over."* Then he smacked his lips together as in a kiss, turned, put his arms around the two nearest boys, whispered something, and they all laughed as they sauntered off.

"Put away the knife and come with me." She spoke softly but in a tone that informed Marcus he had no choice. By the time they reached the band rehearsal room, her nerves from the conflict had settled.

"Look around. I believe you're Marcus Darby. I'm Ms. Nichols, the band director and your neighbor."

"I know who you are," he sullenly replied as he wandered the space filled with chairs, musical instruments, music stands, and shelves of stacked sheet music. The room had always reeked of orderly disorder. Allie had imagined his mother, the wearer of a mask of serenity, to be the perfect housekeeper, even compulsive. She wondered whether he found the room disconcerting or stimulating.

He explored, tapping hard on a drum, sharply depressing a piano key, and carelessly running his fingers along various instruments. Allie carried two cases to her desk. As he moved about the room, his eyes cut over to where she was lifting an instrument from one of the cases. She fitted and adjusted the mouthpiece on her saxophone. Then she reverently brought it to her mouth and began to play.

Marcus sank into the closest chair. The music Allie played was at first soothing and polished, then raw and emotional. It was interpretative jazz. She focused on anger, distrust, and isolation that transitioned into long plaintive but fading notes, leaving Allie as empty as she sensed Marcus to be.

When she stopped, he shrugged as if to say, *"So, you're the music teacher. Of course, you can do that."*

"Want to try?" she asked, gesturing to the other case. He shook his head, refusing eye contact. "You don't know how to play, so you can't make a mistake." No response. "This is my second-favorite instrument. Number one on my hit list would be the drums. However, I see you on the alto saxophone—maybe because we need another sax player in the band."

"No thanks!" he grumbled, kicking the chair in front of him.

"Let's talk about it, Marcus."

"No thanks," he repeated.

"Here's your choice," she said softly, but showing no sympathy. "You can give me the chance to introduce you to music, or you can report to the principal's office for bringing a weapon to school and drawing it on another student."

Chapter Thirty

Ray felt nauseated when she heard Allie's version of the story, thinking of her with a knife at her back as she faced a bully easily twice her size.

"Will any of them talk about it?"

"I don't think so. There's nothing to brag about."

"Well, it sounds like you have just made some enemies and taken on the responsibility of a messed-up teenage boy. I hope he has some musical talent. Did you confiscate the knife?"

Allie handed the blade to Ray, who immediately handed it back.

"Here. Take it. Maybe it should live in your backpack for self-defense."

"Ray, can you picture me stabbing someone?"

"I don't want to." She sighed deeply as she made a decision of her own. "So, hide it. Give it back when he graduates."

She didn't want to think the bullying had been so physical that Marcus actually felt the need for self-defense. This led her to wonder how many times there had been a pre-planned or accidental death at a school because someone brought a weapon, maybe because someone had felt threatened. She actually went to her computer and was surprised by the data.

The mass shootings that terrified society in recent years were usually committed by an adult coming into a school and killing randomly. The exceptions were the Colorado shooting when two boys killed fifteen, and the Minnesota shooting by one boy who killed ten.

Could their own small-town bullies actually become so passionate they would create more than mischief?...Or could their victims?

After the knife incident, Ray decided it was time to follow Allie to school again—like she was still in kindergarten. Only a person whose mind was so narrowly focused would make such a choice. Only a person who lived on the fringe, as Ray did, could make such a choice and get away with it.

"I would like to help with the band more, Allie."

"You're pretty busy with your own work and college classes, Ray."

"Not really. I've been asked to work nights at the hospice center, and my only class is in the morning."

"So, when would you sleep?"

"Before and after Band. You know me, I don't need much sleep."

"All right, I could use your help. I'll ask about it."

"No problem. I've already asked." She pulled out an ID card and clipped it to her shirt pocket. "They were happy to get an unpaid teacher assistant."

Ray not only helped with the band class and practice; she also monitored the hallways between classes where bullies were likely to transgress. When she began to feel like a stalker instead of a bodyguard, she stayed home—embarrassed and confused by her own behavior.

Sometimes, a peacefulness came over her, and she felt no need to keep an eye on her cousin, or Marcus, or the bullies. On those days, regardless of weather, she wandered the waterfront, read the names of the boats, and imagined where they had been and where they might go.

Marcus's schedule was adjusted to include Band, and Allie gave him private lessons twice a week after school. The cousins often sat on the front porch of their home and listened as, across the street, Marcus struggled for clarity of sound in the music language so new to him. But once they heard clear beautiful notes, they knew he was hooked, and they also heard the sound of a life changing.

The first person in the band to make an effort to communicate with the reclusive Marcus was Katie, a member of the drumline. She was small, almost pixie-like with short, curly blonde hair, twinkling green eyes, and mischief all over her face. Much to her chagrin, her nickname was Tinkerbell. In her uniform, with her snare drum, she looked like something that should be miniaturized and hung on a Christmas tree.

"Yo, Marcus!" she said in a nonchalant tone while tapping her drumsticks on a folding chair next to her. It was a subtle invitation to sit.

"Marc," he corrected.

"Yeah, Marcus does sound like a Roman soldier ready to crucify Christians—also sounds kinda stiff, doesn't fit. I think you're cool. Your horn's really improving."

Taken back, Marc sat in the proffered chair and gave his rare smile. "Do you always come on so strong?"

"Never. But you're different. We can be friends." She held up a fist and he bumped it.

Ray watched the two with envy as she set up the folding chairs and music stands. How simply they connected and how comfortable they became with seemingly no effort or doubt about the rightness of it. Allie also heard their conversation as she reviewed the day's music at her desk. From that moment on, Marcus became Marc.

Chapter Thirty-One

One day Marc walked into Band class with a bruised and swollen bottom lip, blood still wet, the injury fresh.

"I tripped." He refused to make eye contact, then proceeded to pull out his sax. He looked at the mouthpiece and winced in anticipation of the pain to his wounded lip.

"Go clean yourself up," Allie said, nodding at the first-aid kit on the wall. She looked questioningly at Katie, who turned away.

Another girl whispered Mike Harris's name, and everyone sucked air through their teeth.

Allie walked over to Marc at the sink, rinsing his mouth. "You aren't carrying a knife or other weapon of mass retribution, are you?"

He snorted a laugh and winced again.

Allie left Ray in charge of setting up the room for practice and went in search of Mike Harris, the smallest but apparently one of the most aggressive of Buck's followers. A call to the front office had revealed where he would be during that class period.

Allie looked through the glass in the door to identify Mike. All heads were down as they took a quiz, but his red hair gave him away. She stopped her hand on the doorknob and leaned her head against the glass. All of them bent to their task, trying to find an answer in their memory or on a neighbor's paper. It was both touching and humorous.

Ray knew there would be no confrontation that day. She walked up to Allie and put her arm around her. "Marc has the class," she whispered. "He's leading since he can't play with that lip."

Allie released the doorknob and turned. "I remembered one of the times I was bullied. It made me question what might have happened today.

"In middle school, a girl older and larger than me pushed

me down after someone else pushed her. My backpack fell as well as my glasses, both then kicked around on the hall floor. Everyone nearby gathered to watch and laugh. I looked up into the other girl's face, and asked her 'Why?' The girl's returned glance held both regret and shame. But she walked away without a word.

"A black girl from my English class offered her hand, then helped me pick up my things. 'Why didn't you hit her back?' she asked me.

"I said, 'I didn't want to.'

"'She'll do it again, especially if it makes the other kids laugh. Don't you know? They won't hurt you unless you let them.'

"I wonder if Marc fought back—and if Mike accidentally tripped him or did it to get someone's attention, or approval, or laughter.

"But the teacher in me just could not interrupt a test."

Together, they walked back to her class.

"So, are you going to confront him?" Ray asked after the day was over and the room had emptied.

"You know how I am about confrontation. I can always find a reason to avoid it. But this time I will follow protocol and contact the school counselor."

"Good for you."

Minutes later, Allie nervously addressed the counselor, not in person but on the phone. "Mike Harris?" Alicia Raven asked. "He might have tripped the Darby boy, but Buck Bailey was probably behind it. Mike is his follower."

"So, what do we do?"

"I don't know, Ms. Nichols. A busted lip is minor. And I have little power. Right now, I spend my time trying to write up a dress code that the students and parents are likely to follow and advising college-bound students. You can't limit skirts to inches because the same length looks fine on some body types and whorish on others." Allie didn't laugh.

"Seriously," she continued, "the bullied kids don't come to me—probably afraid. If you can create a strategy that curtails Buck's or Mike's behavior, I'll certainly be happy to hear it."

A week later, another of Allie's students came to band class with a black eye. He refused to discuss it, but after class, Katie told her it was Mike Harris again....

"Mike, the little one?" Allie asked.

"Yes—little but mean."

"Tell Ray I'll be back. Start class without me."

Allie again called the office to determine where Mike would be. This time she would not let sentimentality or memories get in her way.

Allie poked her head inside the room and asked politely to speak with Mike. There was no one in the hall to observe what happened—at least not when she looked. Soon after Mike came out, another kid exited the men's room across the hall. He paused when he saw Ms. Nichols close the door behind Mike and then whirl on him, grab the neck of his t-shirt and pull his face close to hers. Her drumstick, always on her person, was in her other hand. She pushed the tip against his chin, forcing it up so they were eye-to-eye.

"You little bastard!" she growled in a stage whisper. "You touch a hair on the head of any one of my students again and your balls will be decorating my drumsticks! Do you understand? And, if you tell anyone what I just said, I'll call you a liar and find a way to get you suspended—permanently! Do you understand that?"

Without making a sound, he nodded his head and covered his wet crotch with his hand. She released him and opened the door for him to resume his detention. But he slipped past her and ran to the restroom. The other boy ducked around the corner to begin the urban legend of what he had witnessed.

Allie's face reddened and she trembled with regret. She had just bullied a student. But it had seemed the only way to get his attention, perhaps the only behavior he understood.

Chapter Thirty-Two

When Allie met Marc, he was no taller than she. When his sophomore year began, his feet were well below his band uniform.

Ray wondered if his bones ached from their ongoing stretch. It was difficult to eat enough calories to keep up with such growth, and his newfound thinness as well as height made him look almost frail.

The other band members made playful jokes about "the evolution of Marc" but, like Ray, they realized his increasing height simply made him stand out in the crowded halls, a more easily identified target. They began walking with him to classes as a kind of human buffer.

As usual, Ray watched both the musicians and the audience in the orchestra performance. She actually heard sighs from the girls sitting nearby, saw them swooning when Marc rose and played a solo. Even the girls in the band seemed to lean towards him when his soulful music filled the room. Ray made mental bets with herself about when one of them would actually fall off her chair.

He is oddly attractive for a skinny horn player, but his music is even more attractive.

Marc and Katie sat outside on the steps of the main classroom building one morning, waiting for the bell to call them inside. Nearby, Ray enjoyed the sunshine and tried to read her book. Instead, she shamelessly listened to their conversation. They were arguing. There had been another encounter with Buck in the hall during lunch break the day before.

"Ms. Nichols asked me to run an errand..."

"And you ran into Buck and the devil's twins, Thing One and Thing Two. What happened?"

"Nothing, just shoved me around and said stupid stuff. Everyone found it funny."

"Like what?"

His face clouded with the remembered ugly words, the rude clowning, and the laughter. He forced a smile. "Like how lucky I am to have you for a girlfriend."

She didn't challenge the obvious lie, but said, "I'm taking a self-defense class at the Y after school. You should come."

Marc ducked his head to hide the blush. "I have work after school—you know that."

"Okay, how about a compromise," she offered. "Dad used to box—golden gloves. He could teach us both—on your schedule. I've avoided that because I don't like hitting my own dad. However, if you are there to be my sparring partner, I could hit you, not him. And he would be thrilled because he could save the cost of our Y membership. Perfect."

Marc's dark hair fell over his forehead as he studied his shoes. Then he slowly lifted his head, blue eyes sparkling. "I don't know. Will you go easy on me, Tinkerbell?"

"Dude! Not a chance." She shoved him sideways.

He sat up and pulled her closer, then quickly kissed her surprised lips. "Okay," he laughed when she kissed him back. "YOLO, let's do it."

"No," Katie laughed. "It isn't 'you only live once.' Snoopy got it right when he told Charlie Brown, 'You only die once. You live every day.'"

Ray put her book away and thought of Mary and all the days she hadn't lived.

Chapter Thirty-Three

Bullying existed on social media as well as in the school halls and bathrooms. Online activities were mostly malicious character assassinations—which could lead to serious consequences. Abuses seemed to grow along with the technology.

One day someone sent Allie a message with a website link—a YouTube address.

She reluctantly brought it up and watched with Ray at the kitchen table. They both gasped aloud when the computer screen showed Buck push Marc into an empty classroom. It had to be the drama rehearsal room because the chairs were all moved to the side and the floor had tape on it to represent a ground plan for location of scenery and props.

Other boys followed. They jostled and laughed as testosterone overcame years of parental guidance. The door closed and the two adversaries faced each other within the circle of onlookers. Marc tried to leave, but the circle tightened and someone pushed him to the center where Buck waited, grinning and clowning.

Marc moved sideways, probably hoping to get closer to the door. Buck also stepped sideways, bent over, leered, made teasing half-lunges. When the blackboard was at Marc's back, Buck stopped, then rushed at him, pushing him against it. The circle of onlookers scattered. Marc recovered, ducked a punch and moved surprisingly fast, shoving Buck as he jumped back into the center of the room. Buck made an exaggerated fearful response, bringing laughter from the observers. But the game had changed; the kid had fought back. Buck's face changed from mocking to ugly as the cruel words fell from his twisted mouth.

"He's the son of a pervert," Buck announced to his audience. "I hear he's the same—likes doing the Stick and Tinkerbell at the same time."

"Maybe he watches while they do each other," someone else offered. More laughter echoed.

Marc lunged for his tormentor, but someone tripped him, and he landed at Buck's feet. Not expecting this, Buck jumped back, out of Marc's reach. Then he dropped to all fours, like a panther about to spring. The two were face-to-face.

The last words of the video that would go viral were more of a hiss than a voice, "I hear your old man raped a thirteen-year-old girl."

Before Marc could refute Buck's words or exact a revenge, the door opened and a teacher entered. The video ended.

And now it wasn't just the neighbors or the town who knew about Frank Darby…

Chapter Thirty-Four

For the second time, Allie found the courage to step out of her comfort zone and address the problem directly. She knew better than to confront Buck as she had Mike. Instead, she went to the school counselor in person. Ray followed for moral support.

In the office, Allie dropped her pencil and pad out of nervousness. Ray picked them up. She almost dropped them again when she saw the stunning black woman behind the desk who rose, surprising them with her height and her perfect ensemble: a white cotton blouse tucked into the tiny waist of a bright blue skirt, the perfect length to show her long legs but not so short to be inappropriate.

"I don't get out of the band room often enough. We haven't met." Allie tentatively offered her hand and thought the counselor didn't need a dress code. She just needed to take a picture of herself and write on it, "Dress like this."

After a brief handshake Alicia Raven said, "Sit down, Ms…"

"Nichols."

"I know who you are…and…?" She asked, nodding at Ray.

"Ray Nichols, teacher assistant." Ray responded as they both sat.

Alicia looked at them both closely. "Sisters?"

"Uh, no," Allie responded, "cousins."

"How can I help you?"

"Wha—what can you tell us about Buck Bailey?"

"Buck!" She leaned back in her chair, evaluating Allie and deciding how much she should say.

"His father's an Army sergeant. According to his mother, they followed him from base to base until she finally divorced him and she and her son settled here, near her own mother who passed soon after they arrived. She found work in Greenville and commutes daily, leaving Buck on his own much of the time.

"He has always picked on smaller, weaker boys," she added, "mostly just intimidates, never quite breaks the school rules, much less the law. Unfortunately, we don't have an official policy against bullying.

"His mother is single, and because he often gets into trouble when he's unsupervised, she usually sends him away for summer break."

"To…to where?" Allie stammered.

"A camp, or to her in-laws…or worse—to his dad."

"Have you seen the video?" Allie asked.

"Yes, Ms. Nichols. It is unfortunate. We have no control over what students post on the internet. And we have no idea who videotaped it or who posted it. No rules about that either. But no one was hurt, and Frank Darby's history was never a secret. Marcus's parents have not complained. I've offered counseling for him."

"For whom? Marc or Buck?" Allie demanded. There was silence as Ms. Raven shuffled through papers, obviously just to have something to do while not making eye contact.

"For whom?" Ray echoed.

Alicia looked up and smiled as if she were granting a benevolent favor. "For Marcus, of course. He has to learn how to deal with public attitude towards his father."

"Counseling Marc won't stop the bullying," Allie said through gritted teeth as she found her courage. "What are you going to do, wait until Buck really hurts someone?"

"Right!" Ray agreed. But they were focused on each other, ignoring her. She felt like the comic relief in a serious drama.

"Oh, you want to stop the bullying? Well, good luck. Kids may not speak up, but parents do. And Buck isn't a bad boy. Only one couple has made complaints, and he apologized to them and to their son. I believe he was sincerely sorry. I think his outbursts of anger and his need for control are a result of his father's dominating behavior."

"Does that make it okay? And do you only listen to

parents?" Allie asked with dripping sarcasm. "The whole school watched the fight on YouTube. No one was hurt physically, but it was still excessive. And what about the insinuations?"

"What?"

"The comments about me."

"You? I didn't hear that."

Allie stood and raised her right hand. It held a drumstick, as usual. Alicia visibly shrank.

"The students call me 'Stick' behind my back because I'm a drummer." No longer nervous, she was bent over Alicia's desk. "Everyone knew who Buck meant."

"Well, obviously not everyone," Alicia coughed out, relieved the gesture with the drumstick wasn't a threat, but clearly unable to connect it to the video.

Allie's shoulders sank. She knew not to call attention to even the suggestion of sex with a student—not in today's climate. Teachers were often in the news and in court or litigation for less. Allie made one last appeal.

"You know," she continued, changing the focus from herself, "many children don't tell parents everything—especially when they feel powerless because no one of real authority will help. And bullying has been proven to be a trigger for greater violence in schools all over the country."

"Yes," Alicia agreed, "and more often, the violence comes from their victims."

Alicia rose again to her full height, causing Allie to back away.

"Tell me, Ms. Nichols, has anyone ever bullied you?"

"Yes, when I was a child."

"Have you ever bullied anyone?"

Remembering her threats to Mike, Allie said nothing.

"Sometimes, Ms. Nichols, it's difficult to determine who is the bully and who the victim. Maybe even more difficult to define the act itself."

Satisfied that her recommendation for counseling Marc was the solution needed for minimal fallout, she returned to the paperwork on her desk, silently dismissing Allie and Ray.

As they left, she added, "Because it took place on school property, Buck will be given a warning, Ms. Nichols. The next infraction will lead to a suspension. That's the best I can offer you."

"You know," Allie said as they walked back to the band room, "I knew my own students called me Stick—not to my face, of course. Didn't realize everyone used the name."

"In your classroom, you point to the blackboard or to your students with your stick; you use it to direct the band in practice; you knighted Marc with it after his first concert solo. You nearly drive them crazy, tapping on your desk with your stick while they're taking a quiz."

"But that's just with my students."

"Students talk. And everyone takes your music appreciation class."

"Are they making fun of me?" She had been grinning, but the grin faded and she asked seriously, "I mean, do they think I'm weird?"

Chapter Thirty-Five

Music and band classes were held in an annex separate from the rest of the school. Allie only saw Buck when they shared the same lunch session, as they did the following spring.

She usually ate lunch while catching up on paperwork. Ray sat across from her, forcing down a tuna sandwich. Buck wandered the cafeteria, shoving someone here, pulling a pony-tail there. When seen with the other students, he seemed almost a tease—just trying to get attention. Ray's mouth pulled to the side in confusion as she watched him, almost softening to this unpredictable boy.

"Just when I thought I knew him," she mumbled.

He always made a point of bumping Allie's chair and mumbling an obscenity that only she could hear. Usually she ignored him, but this time she reacted when he kicked her chair in passing.

"Why?" she asked.

"Why what?" he challenged, turning.

"Why do you do these things? What's wrong with you?"

"Nothing!" he flared. "What's wrong with you?" The clown face turned ugly. "I hear you're nuts, Stick!"

The look of hurt on her face was his reward. Nearby students turned and stared. Ray started to rise, but Allie signaled to her to stay in her chair.

"I was, once." she responded softly, regaining composure, "after my mother died. I got help, some professional…but most from family and a friend. I'm fine now."

Buck paused, surprised by her admission. Just as quickly, he recovered, leaned down, and hissed in her ear, "Yeah, Stick. You are so-o-o fuck-in' fi-n-n-n-e…" stressing and elongating the last word with all the sexual insinuation a sixteen-year-old could muster. Then he laughed, kicked her chair again and pretended he had tripped. He made a clownish attempt to right himself and looked at Allie like he feared her—like she had caused him to fall.

"So sorry, Ms. Stick…uh, uh, I mean Ms. Nichols." His exaggerated apology and obvious sarcasm as he stumbled away pulled laughter from the students who hadn't seen or heard the full encounter. Someone reached out a hand to help Buck as he appeared to stumble again. It was a part of his act, and the helpful hand was an irritant. He shoved the boy aside and strode out of the cafeteria, his middle finger waving above his head.

Ray gripped the table with an unchewed bite of sandwich in her mouth and wished for something to throw that would hurt him as much as he hurt others. She wondered why Allie wanted to understand this demon child.

"That poor boy," Allie whispered and returned to her paperwork.

But Ray could see she was shaken. They had learned to control their walking, to avoid the skips and spins that drew attention. They had also learned to be conventional in other ways, at least in public. Their reputations of being crazy had haunted them from childhood. Small towns, they had learned, could be short-sighted but have long memories.

The year of the video ended, talk about it replaced by other atrocities unrelated to Allie's band. Her students breathed a sigh of relief when Buck went to his uncle's farm for the summer. Surprisingly, Marc went to the counseling sessions.

Chapter Thirty-Six

In the fall, Buck returned with more muscles, a deep tan, and a darker anger. Hard work…and what else? Allie wondered what his grandfather was like and how the farm animals had fared. She wondered if his father had visited the farm. And she wondered why Buck no longer made eye contact, why his stunts no longer held even a touch of humor.

Walking to her classroom one morning, she saw students fall in his path. Of course, his path seemed to be aimed at congested areas. He didn't touch anyone. They fell getting out of his way or bumped into someone else who fell. It was surreal.

A new pattern seemed to be forming, and she felt an internal alarm begin a low warning.

"Sociopaths," Ray read to Allie that evening from an online site, "are believed to be the result of a childhood trauma or a negative environment in which there might be physical or emotional abuse. They have difficulty forming attachments except to a like-minded person or group. They often have little regard for the risks or consequences of their behavior and can be easily agitated or angered, sometimes resulting in violence."

"Childhood trauma, difficulty forming attachments—except for you, my like-minded person. Hmmm, sounds like me," Allie mumbled.

Ray agreed and continued reading. "Unlike sociopaths, psychopaths are generally thought to be born, not made. They may be the result of a genetic predisposition. From early childhood, they exhibit the same difficulty forming emotional attachments. They instead create shallow relationships used for manipulation to serve their needs or goals. But both sociopaths and psychopaths rarely feel remorse or guilt for the harm they cause."

"Definitely not me," Allie sighed, "But I can see how a sociopath could fall between the cracks. On the surface, the description matches so many kids who simply don't 'fit in.' I wonder though, if deep down inside, Buck feels remorse…So, does he have to be one of these options?

"He has been raised by a single mother. Does anyone know if she's abusive, or if she has an abusive boyfriend? You know, he isn't handsome, but he isn't bad looking either. There's something about him that is both appealing and at the same time off-putting. When he does something funny, to cover his bad behavior, I can see the little boy that just wants attention and approval."

"I wonder what his father's like," Ray said as she closed the computer. "Could Buck's behavior be genetic?" She stretched to ease her back. It had been a long and tiring day, and she was due at the hospice center in a few hours. "Maybe we should meet Buck's mother."

"Maybe *I* should," Allie corrected. "Two people asking about her son might be intimidating."

Ray whistled. "Look at you, Miss Independent, Miss Confrontational."

The next Saturday, Allie went to the used car lot in Greenville where Jane Bailey worked and invited the brightly smiling saleswoman to lunch to talk about her son.

At the restaurant, Jane's shoulders slumped and her smile disappeared. Her first words were a surprise. "What's he done now?"

The hostess seated them and Allie waited until she left to respond.

"Buck seems to be going through a difficult phase. Because his behavior affects others, I wanted to meet you and maybe get to know more about him so we might know how to help him."

Jane smiled. "You have a very roundabout way of saying he's a bully."

"I think there's more to him than that."

The waitress arrived and they ordered. An awkward silence followed. Then Jane slowly began to tell Buck's story.

"His father and I were both raised by parents who thought the only way to control behavior was with physical punishment. His father was worse than mine—still is."

She grabbed a napkin and wiped her eyes before the tears

fell. After another pause and a deep breath, she continued. Allie could see this was not a story easily shared.

"After my husband's belt and fists were used on me a few times, I knew it only created hate and fear. But to be honest, I wasn't any better. I had grown up thinking spankings were the normal way to raise a kid. I spanked him to keep his daddy from doing worse and to keep him from becoming his daddy."

"And did it?"

"Sometimes, but not when I was at work and the Sarge (that's what he wants everyone to call him) treated him like a raw recruit in need of discipline."

She paused again and blew her nose. "One day I saw my boy hitting our dog, saying the same things to the poor dog I had said when I spanked him. All I could think was 'that's how he'll treat my grandchild one day. That's what we've taught him.'

"So, instead of physical punishment for bad behavior, I took things away from him, like his games. Now, I take away his phone or don't let him use the car…I thought it was working. Look, I know my boy's a handful, and I worry. But if you met his daddy, you'd think Buck was a sweetheart. And to me, he is."

"I only see the angry side of him, Mrs. Bailey."

"Please, call me Jane. When Buck was little, he was quiet and fearful because of all his daddy's rules and regulations, and the consequences of breaking them. The Sarge used to threaten to sew lace on Buck's 'panties' if he didn't toughen up. So, my little boy toughened up and eventually stopped caring about the beatings. He hated his daddy, but I'm afraid he's becoming just like him."

Armed with those very telling words and more that followed, Allie built up the courage to speak to the school counselor again on Monday. This time she did not focus on Alicia's new ensemble, even nicer than the previous one. This time she was determined to find a solution to the bullying problem.

"In light of other school tragedies around the country, I'm worried about where Buck's bullying might lead. And worse, he has a gang of followers learning through his example."

"Now, Ms. Nichols, he may just be going through a phase."

"No! According to his mother, his father has been molding Buck's attitude and behavior from infancy."

Unmoved, Alicia Raven continued, "We put him in an art class to let him work out his anger on canvas or clay—and to provide him with an opportunity to make new friends."

"Friends!" Allie takes a breath, controlling her anger. "Yes, I spoke to the art teacher. She's terrified. And he's intimidated the rest of the class. They aren't likely to become his *friends*. Have you seen his paintings? They aren't much better than stick figures, but the subjects are either being hung from a tree, or stabbed, or my favorite—lying in four separate pieces, his artistic interpretation of 'drawn and quartered.'"

"I believe he does that for the shock value. And it's just stick figures on paper—not real victims. Maybe he's working out his aggressions or just acting out. Can I call you Allie?"

"If I can call you negligent."

A shadow passed over the counselor's face. "We're planning on placing each of Buck's current friends in one of your music classes next semester. You know, music soothes…"

"Yes, I know…savage beasts!" Allie breathed deeply, calming. "Fine, put them in my music appreciation class, not in my band room. That's a safe place, and I won't have them there. If they cause problems, they're gone."

"All right," the counselor agreed. "If you can't cope, they can go to a drama class."

Allie left, letting the insult to her teaching skills go unanswered. She knew that drama, art, and music classes were where students who did not do well socially or academically were often sent. Sometimes they were a nuisance; sometimes they blossomed. Those same classes were magnets to the shy and lonely students who found acceptance and tolerance for their differences, or in spite of them.

Ray suggested they consult with Will, now a retired clinical psychologist. His comments to their input made so much more sense than Alicia Raven's or Google's.

"I don't know Buck," Will responded to their concerns, "and I can't analyze someone who isn't a patient—couldn't talk about it if I did. But I can speak in generalities. Too often, when a boy or man is kicked by someone stronger—someone who intimidates him—he will lash out at someone smaller and weaker than himself. I've seen it all too often, not only in schools but also in the workplace, and of course, the home. His mother said it. She spanked him, so he spanked the dog."

"But," Ray challenged, "some of us do the opposite of our parents. We don't want to be anything like them."

"And you've succeeded, Ray. But you were never like your mother, and Allie was never like her mother. You two raised each other without their influence and are better for it. It's different with Buck. I'm sure he dislikes his father, and even though he's no longer in his life, maybe the boy still wants his father's approval. And to get his approval, Buck imitates him."

"Can that cycle be broken?" Allie asked.

"With counselling, or sometimes just in the process of maturing. The risk, however, is whether he will reach that level of maturity before something irreversible happens. Teenagers often don't confide their problems, much less their actions, to an adult—not even to a loving parent or teacher. So, their issues can build up in their minds as unresolvable and sometimes unforgivable. Their desperation can lead to terrible consequences. And, by the way, the same can be said of their victims. They can become aggressive or suicidal—or both."

Allie and Ray looked at each other.

Was he talking about Buck or Marc?

Chapter Thirty-Seven

The fall semester brought some relief. Allie and Buck had different lunch schedules, and she only saw him at all-school functions, like pep rallies. When she sat in the bleachers, she could feel someone watching. And if she looked around, she would find Buck, who quickly looked away.

She confided this to Ray, "I swear, even though he tries to pass it off as intimidating and sometimes sexual, I believe Buck wants something more from me."

Ray thought for a moment and then responded. "If you offer him help, what do you think he would do?"

"He would probably misinterpret my intentions. I'm not sure he knows what he wants. There just seems to be some kind of magnetic pull between us, and when it doesn't give me the creeps, it makes me very concerned about him."

"Like Will said, maybe he will eventually mature enough to see the wrong in his behavior, to make better choices, to become the man he is capable of being—not his father."

Then Brandon James, a transfer student known to everyone as BJ, was admitted, and everything changed. He and Buck seemed to become instant friends.

Allie had hoped it would be a positive change for Buck—until she learned the reason for BJ's transfer. He had been expelled from his former school for bullying. Buck had found not a real friendship but a like-minded ally. She saw BJ as a shorter, more handsome version of Buck. She didn't see the major difference. BJ was smarter, more calculating. He spoke, encouraged; Buck acted.

When they walked the hall, it was like the Red Sea parting. Everyone stepped aside. No one wanted their attention. And no one had the courage to stand up to them except Marc.

Just before Christmas, Marc missed the final two days of classes. Ray walked by his house and saw him on the porch with his father, his face purple and blue, one eye swollen shut. She pretended not to notice but slowed her walk, straining to hear their conversation. They spoke softly, in soothing sounds of empathy, encouragement, and affection. Then Marc said loudly, as if mocking himself, "My ninja-like speed earned me a new nickname, 'F'ing Bad Ass.'" Frank laughed, also clearly making light of a painfully serious situation.

When Ray told Allie about Marc's battered face, she all but flew across the street, forgetting her coat. At her arrival, Frank rose and walked into the house. Marc looked down, as if he could hide the damage on his face.

"Was it Buck?" she simply asked. "And where did the fight take place?" Her final question was, "Did anyone witness it?"

After a short time, she returned with a shaky smile and her arms wrapped around herself for warmth, mumbling the story.

"Marc looks bad, but he said Buck has a broken nose and just as many bruises. It seems my boy has been learning to box... with his girlfriend, Katie. It happened on school grounds, and Katie as well as some others saw it. I'm calling the principal right now. I don't care if she *is* on vacation and if tomorrow *is* Christmas."

Chapter Thirty-Eight

Allie spent the rest of the holidays researching and wording a no-bullying policy. Ray warned her that it would be pored over and rewritten by administrators well above her pay grade. But before the end of the break, it was done, and she mailed a copy to Principal Whiting as well as the county school board.

No-Bullying Policy

(A school's responsibility to create and maintain a safe, civil, respectful, and inclusive learning environment)

Bullying or harassment

When one or more students:

A) physically harm another student or cause damage to a student's property;

B) diminish another student's self-esteem through spoken, written, or online slurs, or through demeaning digital images;

C) use racism, sexism, religious bias, or physical appearance to shame or ridicule another student or student group;

D) create an intimidating or threatening educational environment.

Defending oneself in a physical attack is excusable; retaliation after the fact is not.

If an incident is reported by the victim or by a witness, the complaint will be reviewed by an appointed board composed of faculty and students.

The board, depending on the danger to the victim or the student body, will recommend that the bully be warned, counselled, temporarily suspended, or permanently expelled.

Reporting false allegations will result in the same disciplinary steps.

Chapter Thirty-Nine

Allie's call to the principal during her Christmas Eve dinner ignited a chain of events. The proposed policy was adopted and enacted.

When school began again after the holidays, Marc's face was almost back to its normal color, and Buck began a two-week suspension.

The principal had used Allie's unaltered proposed policy as an emergency guide in responding to Buck Bailey's aggression against Marcus Darby. To justify her actions, she had it published in the town's one newspaper, posted and read aloud in every classroom, and emailed to all parents. She decided the county school board, if they chose, could modify it later.

"Do you think it will make a difference?" Ray asked at the end of the day.

"Katie said some of the kids are just laughing at it. No one wants to be a witness when their testimony might be challenged as false. And no real victims want retaliations from the bullies."

"It's just an initial reaction, Allie. I think they're probably relieved for something to finally be put into words. At least it's a start—maybe a wake-up call."

That evening, many parents called the house and either congratulated or complained to Allie. Everyone seemed to think she had left something out or said something too strongly. She was upset and surprised that everyone seemed to know she had authored the policy.

The next morning, the posted copies of the no-bullying policy had been torn down. In the cafeteria, altered copies were passed around to loud laughter. Some students even stood up and read bits aloud. Some were too coarse to read aloud. They were the favorites.

That afternoon, Ray showed Allie one of her edited policies.

Bucking
No-~~Bullying~~ Policy

(A school's responsibility to create and maintain a safe, civil, respectful, and inclusive ~~learning environment~~)
Beating

Bucking or bruising

~~Bullying~~ or ~~harassment~~

When one or more students:

Eats his lunch

A) physically harm another student or ~~cause damage to a student's property~~;

B) diminish another student's self-esteem through spoken, written, or online slurs, or through demeaning digital images; *unless they're sexy*

C) use racism, sexism, religious bias, or physical appearance to shame or ridicule another student or student group; *they can't help they're ugly and dumb*

D) create an ~~intimidating or threatening educational environment.~~ *World of pain*

Stupid just run like Hell!!!

Defending oneself in a physical attack is ~~excusable; retaliation after the fact is not~~.

If an incident is reported by the victim or by a witness, the complaint will be ~~reviewed by an appointed board composed of faculty and students.~~ *ignored*

The board, depending on the danger to the victim or the student body, will recommend that ~~the bully~~ *Buck* be ~~warned, counselled, temporarily suspended, or~~ *permanently expelled.*

Reporting false allegations will result in ~~the same disciplinary steps~~.

Public hanging

While a teacher was writing on her whiteboard, the classroom door opened, and a trash can filled with burning copies of the policy was shoved inside. The door closed. The perp disappeared.

Chapter Forty

In Buck's absence, students no longer tolerated BJ. Alone, he didn't carry the physical intimidation. When he shoved them, they shoved him back.

A few days later, he was seen with Mike Harris and Buck's other followers in tow. They slouched into the cafeteria, ignored the long line waiting for food, and sat at a table with freshmen. The younger students rose and left their food behind. It was the beginning of a threat that felt darker and more sinister as BJ no longer awaited Buck's return.

When he did come back to school in mid-January, Buck was sporting two freshly blackened eyes and stitches in his upper lip—not from his fight with Marc. The common assumption was that the Sarge had delivered his own style of punishment for his son's suspension—or because his opponent survived. When questioned by administrators, Buck merely mumbled a response, claimed to have tripped and fallen down stairs. But this time there was no clowning, no exaggeration—no humor.

The fight before Christmas could have led to both boys being suspended, but there were witnesses who agreed Buck had started the fight, and Marc merely defended himself. BJ, the real instigator and encourager, had remained in the background.

Allie covertly watched Buck. She knew everyone waited for him to commit the final act that would lead to expulsion. But he pulled back whenever BJ tried to involve him in an act of bullying. So, Mike Harris and the other bullies carried out BJ's new cruelties, and he dared anyone to report their abuses. This time it was Buck who stood in the background and watched.

In late February, BJ's voice was heard in nearby classrooms as he screamed obscenities at Buck who turned and walked away. BJ followed and shoved him against the lockers. Still Buck did not fight. A teacher opened her door to see BJ shove him again. Then Buck used his longer reach to hold BJ back.

"I don't want to hit you, man, but I'm not with you on this."

Security had been called and rounded the corner just as BJ kicked Buck in the crotch. He fell to his knees and rolled over in pain. BJ was suspended. The rift in their friendship was almost as strange as the quiet that followed.

An uneasy sense of calm settled only to be wiped out at BJ's reappearance two weeks later.

Their friendship had a slow restart, but the magnet that drew them together was still there. Only this time it was different. They walked the halls quietly and kept to themselves until spring break. On their return, their heads were shaved, and they wore mirrored sunglasses. They rarely spoke. Students reported to Allie that they had either become super cool—or they were smoking something.

Much of it happened under Allie's radar because the band students had been left alone. She did, however, see how thin and hollow-eyed Buck became. She believed that he knew he was broken but had given up looking to her for help. She tried reluctantly to reach out to him. But her attempts at communication were thwarted by the always-present BJ.

Then Katie and Marc brought their concerns about the computer chatter and the school shooting headlines...and the gun...to the band room.

"We all need to get out of here, Allie. The kids may be right. The band room is obviously some kind of target."

"In a minute, Ray. I have a few more things to finish."

"They can wait!"

"NO, they can't! Go home, Ray, and while you're at it, GET A LIFE!"

Stunned by her words, Ray backed away, but just as stubborn as Allie, she turned to the files on the side wall and began the search for the music Allie had previously asked her to find.

"Get a life," she mumbled. "Fine, but not till I know you're safe." She dropped the sheet of music, bent over to retrieve it, and heard the door open.

Chapter Forty-One

The present

A shot is fired, then three more fill the room with deafening blasts, the room meant for music. Silence now...except for the ringing in my ears. I risk raising and turning my head...No one standing.

Marc slides down the wall to the floor—sitting, a growing red bloom on his white t-shirt. The intruders are both down and unconscious. BJ is on his back, eyes open. Buck lies with his head to the side. A stripe of scalp is missing and a growing pool of blood covers his face.

Rolling away from Katie, who scrambles up, Ray crawls... unable to breathe, unable to think...to where Allie had been before she threw her stick and diverted the shooter's aim from her student to herself.

She's down but conscious. She whispers orders to Katie, the only one on her feet. Feeling helpless and useless, Ray covers the hole in her cousin's chest, blood seeping between trembling fingers. The acrid smell of gunpowder fills her senses and then an indescribable smell of blood and death make Ray lean to the side and retch.

Katie pushes a stack of paper towels against Marc's bleeding shoulder, using his belt to hold it in place. He weakly presses it with his opposite hand. She brings more towels and her father's gun to Allie, as ordered, and then calls 911 on Allie's phone. She leaves, crying.

Chapter Forty-Two

Allie whispers for Ray to say she arrived after the shooting because, as always, she needs Ray. Her cousin, the teacher's aide, won't be diverted and questioned by the police if they believe she wasn't in the room for the shooting and therefore doesn't know what happened.

"Help me," Allie says in a fading voice.

"I don't know what else to do."

"Help me…hold the gun with…with my right hand…and pull the trigger."

"Who are we shooting? Everyone's down, Allie."

"The wall—behind where they stood."

With shaking hands, they do it and then drop the gun. Allie has set up evidence to take the blame for returned fire, to protect Marc.

"You are a survivor!" Ray reminds Allie after it is done. "Don't even look for a tunnel or a light. Stay with me!"

Allie's eyes close, but she responds as Ray speaks—keeping her in the present. Her love for her cousin, who sometimes drives her crazy, doesn't let her give in to a beckoning peace, but she can't keep her eyes open. Pain and confusion are winning the day.

Someone she doesn't know talks to her, but her answers are in her head, not spoken. Somehow, she can't make her mouth work.

She feels lifted and then nothing else.

Chapter Forty-Three

The arrival of the first responders is a muddle of police, paramedics and EMTs. Once they determine the blood on her clothes is not her own, Ray is constantly moved from one place out of the way to another as the business of saving lives ensues. Only one is tagged and bagged. Only one is dead.

A policeman recognizes Ray from her work at the hospice center, and she tells him the story of her late arrival. She then begs him to let her accompany Allie in the ambulance, but he suggests she ride with him instead and pummels her with questions the whole way, making the short ride seem unending. Her ears are still ringing from the gunshots but she can't complain as it would put her in the scene during the shooting. So, she repeats her story over and over.

"I told you I was headed for rehearsal and heard the gunshots…five of them."

"Seriously, Ray? You counted?"

"I'm good with sounds. I can still hear them."

"And you ran inside—where guns were being fired?"

"I didn't say I was smart."

"Smart-ass," he amends, only slightly under his breath.

We should have seen this coming. We should have left. There's nothing smart about me—not even my ass.

In the ER, Ray is excluded from everything but the uncomfortable waiting room and white corridors where she sits, paces, and waits for word from the surgeon.

Chapter Forty-Four

The media clamors outside the hospital doors, wanting admission and interviews—with anyone—because no one knows yet exactly what happened. They only know that the band director cancelled rehearsal at the last moment, and in a room where there would have been one hundred musicians, there had only been four. Now three are shot and not yet interrogated; the fourth is dead. No names have been released.

A nurse stands outside the entrance to the hospital, having a smoke during her break. A short blonde girl steps up beside her, interrupts her privacy.

"Could you give this to the Stick—I mean, Ms. Nichols?" She offers the cell phone and looks around before mumbling, "I found it in her classroom." Then with all the anxious fear she has been holding in, she asks, "Do you know if she's okay…and the others?"

The nurse looks down at the young pretty face, twisted with worry. She accepts the cell phone and hesitates before she answers. "Your teacher will be all right. Do you know anything about the shooting? Should you be talking to the police?"

"No, I just know how lost I would be without my phone."

"Right. Do I need to use this to call your parents?"

"No ma'am."

"How did you know Ms. Nichols was hurt?"

"The news did say one person was dead and three injured. It was the band room, and she's always there. It just didn't say who else was there. Most of the band is at the school gym… holding a kind of vigil…until we know what happened and how Ms. Nichols…and the others…are…" She avoids eye contact, hoping the nurse can't see she's lying…that she was there…that she knows who's dead.

"I'm afraid you'll have to wait for the radio or television news to learn more. They aren't letting any information out until the families are notified. Apparently, some are out of town. You should go home and wait until morning. I have to go inside. What's your name?"

"Katie." Reluctant to give her last name, she adds, "She'll know."

Chapter Forty-Five

Semidarkness, middle of the night. Ray sits in the visitor's chair away from the hospital bed in room 314, giving Allie breathing space. She watches the monitors, wills them normal…wishes away the ringing still in her ears.

The door eases open. A doctor enters and goes to her bedside. Ray can't breathe. Ringing gets louder; repeated phantom gunshots—each imaginary bullet explodes in her heart…She knows him!

Knew him…Why is he here? He's a cardiologist, not Allie's surgeon.

Looking away, fearing her eyes will draw his, make him notice her…when all she's wanted for most of her life is for him to notice her again.

Does he remember Allie—when she was a baby—when he carried her in his arms, an infant full of smiles and laughter? Does he remember himself, a slender, handsome boy—and me, a skinny woman-child with tangled hair and heart?

He doesn't even look at the monitors or take any vitals.

He knows she's stable—will survive. It's not her injury that brought him here.

He touches her hair, then turns away…leaves.

The ringing continues. It grows louder.

He remembers and knows who she is! I can feel it….

Ray sighs, then reminds herself of the immediate need to communicate with Allie before the police arrive. She slides her chair closer, whispers, coaxes Allie awake from her hiding place in the netherworld of anesthesia.

"Come out, come out…wherever you are. Allie, Allie, run home free."

Eyes move under delicate lids.

She's in there, somewhere.

One eye opens and Ray is awash in memory. One eye.

If I could go back to that first day, to that pirate baby with only one eye open, what would I do differently? Would she have been safer adopted, raised by strangers? How many times have I asked this question?

Her other eye opens, and the memory of the infant fades.

"Oh, Allie, my cousin, my child, my friend. Take a card, any card. They're all yours."

Allie sees Ray and closes her eyes again. "I thought...you gone."

"Do you want me gone? I think the last time we spoke, before this happened, you told me to get a life."

"Water?"

Ray grabs the lidded container with a bent straw and brings it to Allie's lips. She lifts her head to sip and then lies back.

"...a joke...don't...leave me." Tiny words, barely breathed through the oxygen mask.

Trying for casual, as if yesterday had never happened, Ray waits, afraid, her head still full of memories of Allie's life...

Don't think it was a joke, Allie. We've depended on each other too long. You were just the first to realize it.

She leans forward, chin resting on her hands at the edge of the hospital bed. She's hopeful as she watches and waits for reality to raise its ugly head.

Allie shoves the mask to the side with the hand not encumbered by needles and tubes. She takes tentative breaths, resists panic. Unsure, confused, her large brown eyes search for focus, then suddenly widen in alarm. "What happened?" Reality slowly seeps in.

"Bullet! Upper left side of your chest. And that's a tube between your ribs for draining fluid or something."

In my mind, gunshots pierce the air again, but the ringing is lessened by the joy of hearing her voice.

"Oh." Relief, then doubt, then silence, finding the

pain—deciding how much she really wants to know. "Am I dying?...Where's Marc?...Where's my stick?"

She's back—not just awake, but present, or semi-present, but that's enough.

"You're in Grace Hospital, Allie. You'll be fine. Marc will be fine."

And your stick is on the band room floor.

"Buck," she whispers.

"Will also be fine."

She hasn't asked about BJ...probably already knows.

Allie rolls her head and looks at Ray, who is just a blur without her contacts or glasses. But her cousin is a blur to most people who bother to look.

"Are you in pain?" Ray asks.

"No...yes...not bad." Her head turns again, searching.

"What do you want?"

But Allie follows the pattern of her life, pushes reality away, allows herself access to another place.

"...drum...marching." She pauses, taking a shallow breath, "beat..." She pulls random words as she avoids truths, buries memories, reaching instead for her sounds—her music.

And that's on me! Ray swallows. *It's a learned behavior, and I've been her teacher. Run away from grief.*

But Allie's random words call to both of them: grassy fields, brilliant instruments, and earnest young marchers creating patterns through harmony, contrast—movement and music becoming one. Ray blinks the slate clean, the slate filled with Allie the student, Allie the musician, Allie the teacher.

Ray's eyes move again to the sterile white ceiling. She wonders if God is up there, looking back. What would God see? Two women, the same, but not. Ray is a neutral; Allie, a study in contrasts: her eyes larger, her hair darker, her skin brighter, her feet longer. Once bullied and teased, she is now envied and admired.

She knows Allie will have to answer questions about the

shooting, but she needs to remember more than the trauma that brought her here. Yesterday brought home to Ray the realization that there are no promises of tomorrows for either of them. Facing recent realities may dredge up long hidden memories, easily misinterpreted…inevitably devastating.

A noisy medical cart passes in the hall and pulls Ray back to the present. A chill slowly creeps down her spine. Her always overactive intuition is now travelling at the speed of light.

How many of the gang of bullies might be wandering the halls tonight? Or are they all cowering somewhere, as shocked as everyone else by what happened—trying to distance themselves? They are, after all, only boys.

Chapter Forty-Six

The marching band and color guard fill half the high school gymnasium floor. In the bleachers and also wandering the gym floor are cheerleaders, students, some faculty, a few parents, police at the entrances—everyone sad or angry or both. Everyone tired.

The drum major leads a quartet in a melody from this year's competition theme, "Superheroes: Family and Friends."

Mike Harris, his red hair standing on end, enters and covertly searches the room. He sees his four friends, slouched on the bleachers, isolated from the larger groups. He casually walks over and throws himself onto a seat.

"He's dead!"

"Who's dead?" The Carlson twins sit forward, eyes large.

"BJ."

John Perry, the larger of the four, shoves him hard and whispers, "Shut up, Shrimp!"

Mike flinches at the hated name created and imposed by BJ.

"No one's supposed to know what happened—who's shot, who's dead, nothin'! Less the cops think we know, the better… Damn!…BJ's dead…How'd that happen? I thought they had all the friggin' firepower!"

"I sneaked into the hospital," Mike boasts. "I listened around. I know Buck is down but not dead. So's the Stick," he adds and spits on the floor. "So's that asshole Marc."

"Stay away from the hospital!" mutters Larry Green, the fourth boy, as he sips from a water bottle, then shakes his head to clear it. "You'll get us all involved."

"We weren't there!" the twins say in unison. "But we knew!" Larry swears, then whispers, "BJ was a druggie…off the freakin' grid."

"So what?"

"So, plenty," John growls at the twins, ending the discussion.

"We weren't there, and we knew nothin'! Understand?"

Mike rises. Finally, he feels taller than the others, sees them for the cowards they are. He shuffles over to a freshman cheerleader and whispers in her ear, "You're a tasty snack."

"Creeper!" she mutters and moves away from him to another member of her cheer squad. They both look back at Mike with disgust.

His face reddens and he returns to his friends and their jeers. He takes the water bottle from Larry and chugs the uncut alcohol.

"Hey, 'sup Romeo?"

"So, she's queer for the other one," Mike growls, choking. "What is this stuff?"

Larry smirks. "My daddy said it's 180 proof. Don't strike a match near it."

The twins grab for the bottle as everyone laughs and tries to hide or forget their very real fears.

"So, what do we do now?" Mike asks.

"NOTHING! Leave it alone, Shrimp."

"Fuck that!...And fuck you!" Mike flips them the finger and walks away.

Chapter Forty-Seven

Allie looks at her arm for a watch that isn't there. "What time, Ray?...lost without my phone."

"It's one o'clock in the morning," Ray sings to her, "and it looks like it's gonna be another sleepless night."

"Maybe for you." Allie smiles, sighs, and closes her eyes, trying again to escape the almost-memories as Ray wishes to escape the knowledge of her almost-death. If that bullet had been a touch lower, her Allie would be gone. A familiar rush of survivor's guilt washes over her.

Allie's eyes open. "Why is it so late?...How long have I been here?"

"A long time. You woke up in recovery after surgery, screaming. They gave you something to make you sleep longer, afraid you would tear stitches or something. It was good. They told the cops to go home, that you wouldn't be alert enough for questioning until morning. But they left a guard in the hall. He's supposed to call when you wake up."

The sound of a cart in the hallway. It stops at Allie's door.

"Pretend you're asleep," Ray whispers as she returns the glass to her tray and backs away to the dimly lit corner, remembering she's not supposed to be here. The doorknob turns and a nurse enters the room, shaking her head and clucking in disapproval.

"It's past time for you to wake up but also past time for your medication." She injects something into a tube attached to Allie's arm. "I suppose you need your rest. You did good yesterday, and you'll have to face the morning soon enough."

She's talking to her...knows Allie's awake, but allowing her time rather than alerting the guard.

The nurse starts to leave but turns back, taking something from her pocket. "I almost forgot. A little blonde thing—think her name is Kathy...or no...Katie—caught me on my break. She said this is your phone, and asked me to give it to you. The police wouldn't let her in the hospital, much less your room." She puts it on the tray beside Allie's bed, then leaves on silent shoes.

I like her. And more importantly, Katie's all right.

"We don't have much time, Allie. Can you stay awake a little longer? I need to help you remember some events in your childhood. I know, that's a lot to take in. But trust me, it's important. What is your earliest memory?"

"Mmm, so tired. Don't know…banging a spoon…to make music."

"You did that from the time you could hold a spoon until you finally took drum lessons. Is there a negative memory?"

Allie pauses before responding. "The crash."

"What do you remember about that?"

"Too tired, Ray. Can't think…and don't want to."

"Okay—something less traumatic. What about school?"

Allie begins a slow smile. "I remember Mary."

"What Mary? You mean your mother?"

"Yeah…used to whisper in my ear…when I started school…and the other kids were mean."

"Allie…"

"I know, Ray…She had already left…gone to a better place," she adds with a touch of sarcasm.

"But she whispered in your ear?"

"…told me old knock-knock jokes…made me laugh and feel brave."

"Do you still see her?"

"No…never saw her…just heard her." Allie laughs softly. "…less and less…loved school and learning…spite of mean kids."

"So, even with the bullying, school was a good memory?"

"Yes, Ray…It's why I'm a teacher."

Allie sleeps, and Ray thinks about Mary, feeling a little

wistful, wishing she had heard her, too.

I could have used some knock-knock jokes in those months after the crash.

"Raynelle," Allie chokes as she wakes. Ray jumps, finds her water glass and again brings the straw to her lips. She looks confused, still unsure of where she is and why.

"You were talking about Mary earlier."

"Yes…Mary…She wouldn't let me call her Mama." She pauses. "I never got her…her need to control."

"She didn't know how to be a mama, Allie. The word wasn't in her vocabulary. Her own mother died when she was a toddler. And she was barely sixteen when you were born. Maybe having you and keeping you was her only shot at control."

"You, barely a teenager…called you…Mommy Rayray."

As the medication takes effect, all the tension that had been building is released, and Allie relaxes into a deeper, memory-free world.

Chapter Forty-Eight

Ray knows Allie will have to sleep off the drugs. She moves away from the bed, gently opens the door, and peers at the nurse's station—empty. This is the last of three patient rooms clustered at the end of the hall, rounding the corner, creating a triangle. Ray can see both of the other doors from Allie's room. In front of Buck's room, a city policeman sits in a chair, fighting sleep, playing games on his cell phone.

A security cop rounds the corner and glides by on a Segway—bizarre, surreal. Ray almost laughs, remembering the movie about a mall cop. But hospital security is no joke, and that privately hired policeman on wheels carries a gun. This is his domain, not a temporary assignment, not a comedy on film. Oddly, this makes her feel Allie is safe, at least for the moment.

The cop nods his head and gives up, falling asleep. Ray passes by, noting Buck's door is closed. She looks into Marc's room. He's alone. She wonders why his parents aren't there. The sadness and remorse in the very air from his room make her slip away, around the corner where the cop won't see her if he wakes.

She leans against the wall and wonders how many family members, friends, and lovers have done the same, wearily waiting. By squinting her eyes, she can almost see them—the long line of multicultural, multigenerational leaners—angled pillars holding up these sterile walls.

She suddenly stands up and decides to go home for some necessities, for a shower, for clothes not covered in blood, and for Allie's glasses to replace the contacts removed before surgery.

The media are camped outside the hospital, banned from entering until the victims have been questioned and relatives notified. Someone walks out with a portable microphone to give an update on the condition of the wounded. Ray listens as she hurries by, not wanting them to notice her or her bloody clothes.

Everyone stable. She knew that, but verification is always welcome. The reporters listen and text through the warm night in humidity so thick they could drink the air.

Ray's skin soaks up the damp like a cloak of moisture, relieved to be away from the remnants of violence. Home isn't far. And the walk feels good after the hours of sitting or pacing. Visible in the streetlights, their old place in the Historic District now looks as pretty as the equally ancient Victorians that sit next to it, like sisters in pastel gowns. It's much improved from the shabbiness they inherited so many years ago. What began as shame is now Ray's pride.

The first house on the corner is the tallest, painted yellow with white trim and black shutters—Will and Ranny's home.

Perhaps because their relationship has stood the test of time, and maybe because the times have changed—even here—Will and Ranny have been embraced by the surrounding society. In fact, gay couples are common and hardly noticed. And as retirees from all over the country have moved to this inner-coastal river town, there is a more cosmopolitan segment that has helped to modify old prejudices.

At her own house, Ray looks up to the attic window. A single nightlight allows a glow of warmth and welcome. Ray and Allie have shared that attic room since she was born and remain there now, even though the second floor, with bedrooms once inhabited by Carla and Mary, is now vacant.

Maybe she'll sleep in Mary's room when she gets home—so she doesn't have to climb two flights of stairs.

Across the street, less than a stone's throw, is the Darby house—also empty tonight, and for the same reason.

I need to get back. What was I thinking, leaving her alone?

There's mail, a birthday card from Bernie and a postcard from Carla, currently on vacation with Ben. She wonders if Allie even remembers that it's her birthday.

Does Carla know about yesterday? Do the authorities know how to reach her? This postcard has her hotel's address and phone number. Can't draw attention to myself by turning it over to authorities. All of the involved families are being questioned at the police station. Can't talk to them until we have a story.

Allie can call Carla in the morning—no need to wake her

only to cause a night of worry.

After collecting a few of Allie's things, Ray rinses off in the shower, changes from bloody casual clothes and sneakers to a blue sundress that once belonged to Mary, anything to lighten the gloom. Then she rushes back to the hospital through a misty rain.

Chapter Forty-Nine

More students arrive at the gymnasium. The story of the cancelled band rehearsal followed by the shooting was started by members of the band but has already grown out of proportion. So has the noise as everyone seems to talk at once, sharing what they know and reacting. It is no longer the sad, worried atmosphere of a vigil, but an event charged with excitement over what might have been. Some faces look frightened; some look thrilled with the drama; some more tenderhearted cry; some just sit and stare into space. They all respond in their own way to the slaughter that could have happened, the exaggerated numbers of unrealized deaths and injuries. The real wounded seem almost forgotten.

The press interview students. Katie avoids them as she climbs to the top of the bleachers and watches the dynamics of the crowd with wonder and more than a little anger.

Larry, from the isolated group of Buck's and BJ's followers, is trapped between a camera and reporter as he tries to slip into the restroom after he cuts in line and elbows a younger boy out of his way.

"Young man," the reporter calls above the noise of the crowd, "can I interview you?"

"No," he mutters, trying to duck inside.

Curious, Katie moves closer.

The reporter extends her hand with the mic. "Can you tell us what you know about the band rehearsal being cancelled just before the shooting?"

Larry stops and slowly turns to the reporter and camera. He seems surprised at their lack of information. "Yeah, okay. My name's Larry Green...Maybe everyone knew," he responds, taking his time, clearly trying to decide how to reveal what he knows. "It was weird...posted on Facebook in private...or maybe public...that...uhm...something big was going down." He scrambles to add, "But nobody knew where or when."

John Perry grabs him and pulls him to the side while

knocking the camera to the ground and cracking its lens. "You asshole! Shut up! Let's get outta here!"

"Son of a—" the cameraman explodes.

Nearby students pause in their excited conversations, temporarily silenced by the broken camera.

"Hold it, son." Another man has made his way through the crowd. He flashes a badge and quickly pockets it as John turns to run. In only a few steps, he grabs John's arm with one hand and Larry's shirt with the other, stopping them. "Let's go somewhere and talk—both of you."

The crowd has moved back to avoid the action, but remains quiet, spellbound, as word of the conflict spreads.

John tries unsuccessfully to pull his arm away. "Hey, chillax. Don't press me, man. We're just bookin'."

"Pierce!" the detective calls. "Come over here."

A tall policeman in uniform responds, "'Sup, Detective?"

"I think I need a translator and a private space. You look like the youngest cop here."

"Sure, me and these tools are tight," he laughs, putting his arm around Larry. He smiles congenially as he reaches around the other much larger boy and half-carries them both into the men's room while others clear out at the sight of the uniform.

The noise of the crowd resumes with a new excitement as the door closes. Katie chews her nails, something she hasn't done since she was twelve.

In only a few minutes the boys reappear in handcuffs, led by the police, who direct them to the exit. This time, students make space for the bullies, but not out of fear. This time, they are followed by jeers and laughter.

The Carlson twins watch the events from the bleachers. They drop the empty water bottle and then slowly try to work their way around the moving crowd. Both have had too much of the 180-proof liquor. They stagger past and into students until they reach a locker room.

Katie sees them from her higher perch. She quickly descends, losing herself among the band members on the gym floor. Moments later she emerges with two of the musicians who follow her into the same locker room.

Chapter Fifty

It's surprisingly easy to sneak back into the hospital. The police are busy trying to usher what are probably families and friends of other emergency patients into the building while fending off the media. There aren't many because of the early morning hour.

Ray sees a girl she met at the hospice center, a visitor. She wonders if the girl's grandmother Hannah took a turn for the worse and some misguided relative called for an ambulance rather than letting her go peacefully. Ray walks beside the girl, asking about Hannah, and enters the hospital beside her—as if they were together.

On the third floor, she finds Allie still asleep. Refreshed, Ray leans back on the recliner, still trying to decide what to share of the past that might help Allie deal with what happened yesterday and what will happen today.

She can't prevent the image of a fallen Allie holding a gun, too injured to pull the trigger. Ray's own eyes close in self-defense as she too sets aside what she's unwilling to relive.

She again hears footsteps and a medical cart.

As the nurse enters to check Allie's vitals, Ray slips out of the room. She looks in on Buck, whose door is now open and who appears to be sleeping soundly. She sighs at the sight of his restraints and realizes the authorities must know he was one of the shooters. She passes by Marc's room. His mother is there now, holding his hand. Then she sees a tall figure beside the window—his father, Frank Darby—for once not on his porch. They must have been delayed at the police station. Ray shudders at the thought of how the police probably treated Frank.

How long has Marc been defending his father as well as himself? How isolated he must feel surrounded by people—even kids—who assume he is possibly the same as his dad…and who associate his father with guilt even though he was eventually acquitted.

Finding an empty waiting room, Ray sits in a

semi-comfortable chair. She has always been steady energy, so this tiredness, this weight she seems to be carrying, is almost alien. When patients died at the hospice center, it seemed not a tragedy but the natural end to their cycle of life—at least for the elderly. BJ's death, because of his youth and the violence, is still a shock. But her eyelids can't stay open any longer. It feels so good to close them and blot out everything, to welcome the dark.

Moments later, she's surprised when she sees Allie and Buck walking towards her. They're laughing. She invites them into the living room, and they sit, making small talk. There's a hole on the right side of Buck's head. They pretend not to notice. Then Allie asks Buck something, and he turns to her. The left half of his head is missing! Ray involuntarily jerks and cries out.

An old man sitting next to her pats her arm and speaks soothingly. "They'll be all right," he says.

She leans forward, squeezing her eyes closed, trying to push the image from her mind.

Buck has a head wound, but nothing serious—certainly not the horror in my nightmare!

She opens her eyes, hoping light will erase the memory. No one is there, not even the old man.

Lost in thought, Ray wanders down to the floor where pulmonary patients struggle with lung issues ranging from pneumonia to cancer. Most of them are old. Some are awake; some sleep. Some see her and wave or smile; some don't. The clock on the wall says it's four in the morning. Hannah should be here somewhere.

She pauses at the rooms where sleep evades and worry or anticipation have become their focus. They all seem to be on oxygen, getting help with getting breath, with staying alive. As quickly as the thought is born, the words and music of a song fill the space in her mind. She hums and dances down the hall until she finds the door with the name Hannah Steinbach. Softly, she sings.

"Ah, ha, Hannah, stayin' alive…
Got the wings of heaven on my shoes
I'm a dancin' woman and I just can't lose

You know it's all right, it's okay
You'll live to see another day…
You're stayin' alive, stayin' alive
Ah, ha, Hannah, stayin' alive, stayin' alive…"

Her reward is the light in Hannah's eyes as Ray dances up to her bed, softly singing the last words.

"Hey Hannah," she whispers, not wanting to wake the young woman snoozing in the visitor's chair. It's the girl Ray had walked beside as she reentered the hospital. Hannah's grand-daughter was pulled from her bed after a full day at work to this sterile room for this lonely vigil.

From her years at hospice, Ray knows, blessing or curse, when someone's time is almost gone, when hugs and comforting are lacking and most desired. She knows Hannah's time is short.

"My name is Raynelle," she whispers. "Remember me? I remember you from hospice where you sleep all day and stay awake all night." Hannah doesn't speak but follows her visitor with pale blue eyes as she sits on the bed and holds her thin, veined, almost translucent hand.

"What have you loved most in your life?" Ray asks her.

A tiny smile opens her mouth. But still she can't speak because of the oxygen mask and her own weakness. Her eyes move left toward the sleeping young woman.

"Ah, yes. I know all about loving a young person, especially one who loves back—as she does. And what else, Hannah?"

Her eyes slide back to Ray and widen just a little. "Me?" Hannah shakes her head, trying to look down, beside the bed, at Ray's feet.

"Shoes? You're a shoe freak?" Again, the shake of Hannah's head and an almost smile.

"Oh, I understand. You like dancing." The aged head nods and a tear slides down one side of her face.

Ray rises, still holding her hand and begins to hum, then sing, "Stayin' alive, ah, ha, ha, ha…" and as she sings, her feet move. Hannah closes her eyes and pulls the mask away. Her fingers tighten on Ray's, and her shoulders move just a little, keeping time. At the foot of her bed, Ray can see her toes clenching and unclenching, also keeping time.

Hannah was a dancer.

There's a sound from one of the machines and some lights blinking. Ray puts the mask back over Hannah's open but still mouth. Her granddaughter stirs.

"I'd better go," Ray whispers, kissing her forehead before she turns to leave.

A nurse rushes in. Ray finds a chair in the hall and sits, closing her eyes, pondering the "whys" of it all. Finding no answers, she opens them to see a familiar elderly man beside her.

"Hello there," he offers.

"Hello back." Ray looks suspiciously at him. "Didn't you sit beside me on another floor?"

"Oh, I wander."

"Me too. Been here long?"

"Depends," he laughs.

"On what?"

"On what you consider to be long."

A door opens and he rises. "There she is. There's my dancing girl." And the man who comforted Ray after her nightmare about Buck moves with surprising energy to catch up with the gurney carrying Hannah, followed by their weeping granddaughter.

She stands up, watching them leave and hears a deep sigh. A man in a white coat is beside her, also watching the disappearing gurney. His shoulders slump.

"How long have they been married?" she asks, wondering, not expecting an answer., trying to remember what she knew about Hannah.

"She was married for over sixty years—until she lost him about eight months ago," he responds and turns, only glancing at Ray, who gasps as she sees the gurney continue down the hall without the old man. The doctor starts to walk away and stops, turns again, looks at Ray again. She feels his eyes and looks up. It's Hans. And he's noticed her…again.

Chapter Fifty-One

Ray turns to leave, but he's beside her, stopping her, shock and confusion on his face.

"Is it really you? Raynelle, is it you?"

She starts to speak, but covers her mouth with her hand, mute, unable to find words.

"Of course it's you. You look the same. I don't know what to say. I've seen you in my mind so many times...and you're so...unchanged." He pauses as a slight smile of understanding removes the tension in his so familiar, but not quite the same, face. "Oh, of course, you're here because of Allie, Mary's girl."

His face is fuller, with a few frown lines, but still the same kind face she remembers. He wears round glasses, and small wrinkles edge his eyes. He's slender but not the thin boy he had been. His hair is the same as it was, sandy and sun-brightened.

"Yes," she responds weakly.

He blinks. "I have so much to ask you, so much to tell. But I have a brief consult to attend." Frustration evident, he stammers, "Will you meet me in the cafeteria in fifteen...maybe twenty minutes? Please."

She nods but adds, "The café instead, near the entrance."

"All right. If I'm late, don't leave."

Ray knew he had moved back to her town, had sensed him and avoided places where he might be. In crowds, he had never noticed her, but tonight...tonight was different. He saw and knew her, as if twenty-seven years had not passed.

At the café on the first floor, it isn't hard to locate an empty table, one near the doors where he'll easily find her and where she can see the elevators.

For months, she'd put her personal feelings on lockdown, focusing on Allie, on her safety—for all the good that did. She had postponed thoughts of Hans here, Hans—not a distant memory. Hans, a reality. Hans, who saw and instantly knew her.

I have spent so many years living on the fringe, a will-o'-the-wisp, a non-reality to everyone except Allie. I should have run before his eyes and brain connected with what he saw standing beside him. But I was busy watching a ghost follow a gurney. Once again, my crazy imagination betrayed me.

When does one become too old to remember the yearning of youth, label it puppy love, dismiss it as fleeting and of little substance? Only those whose hearts never move beyond that love know its power and its longevity.

"Coffee?" Hans asks as he sits down across from Ray, jarring her back to the present. She had completely missed seeing him enter the cafe. For a moment she panics.

What else have I missed?

"I'm fine. I mean, no thanks."

He puts his cup down and stares, causing her to drop her eyes.

"First, tell me about Allie. I know she'll be all right, but… what happened?"

Ray sighs trying to think what to tell and what to skip. "Allie's had problems with a bully for a long time. In the beginning, he targeted her students, then he targeted her. We thought the problem had eased off, but we were concerned for him. He seemed to change. I don't know…maybe drugs. Two of her musicians came to the band room yesterday to warn Allie about something they saw on the internet. They didn't know what was planned, just that it could become violent. They brought a gun for Allie's protection. Before they could leave, two more boys came in with guns, and now one is dead and three injured."

Ray leaves out the details of the shooting since they haven't decided on their story yet. Wanting to prevent his questions, she segues to another time and story.

"I have a long-overdue apology for you." she says and forces herself to look up. But he smiles, stops her heart…and her confession.

"We both have things to say, Raynelle. I'm still overwhelmed. I don't even know what questions to ask…Do you live here? Have you been here all along?"

"Yes, still in the same house. My mother married and lives out of town now, on the river. What about you?"

His smile broadens. "I've become a kid again, living my dream. I'm on the river too—but on a boat."

"You live on a boat? Where?"

"I used a friend's slip at the Village Wharf last winter. But he's back, so she's docked at the waterfront in town. I sleep here at the hospital half the time."

"I know all the boats at the waterfront. What's her name? Wait…let me guess." She closes her eyes, pictures the boats that haven't been there for long. "There's a trawler out of South Carolina named *Dixie Belle*. It has a confederate flag painted beside its name. Not yours." He chuckles and shakes his head, and Ray continues.

"There's a Boston Whaler named *The Office*. Too small to live on. It looks brand new, and I'll bet the owner's wife doesn't know it exists. When he uses it, he probably says, 'I'm going to the office, dear.'" They both laugh. Then another vessel enters her mind.

"There's a forty-foot sailboat—old, wooden, immaculate." She hesitates, unable to speak the name.

"*Ray of Light*," he says for her. "I remembered watching you and Mary's baby at the docks, twirling in the summer noonday light. Those were probably the happiest days of my life. Raynelle, our time may be limited. If so, I don't want to waste it on small talk. I could be called to attend a patient at any moment."

"And I need to get back to Allie," Ray interrupts. "After yesterday, when I almost lost her, I realized my own mortality and there are things I need to help her remember now because… because she might misinterpret them if I'm not around to explain. And then you appeared, another memory." She shifts in her chair, looks again at the elevators.

"What's wrong, Raynelle?"

"Nothing! It's just time…My time is limited because Allie and I have to decide what she'll tell the police before they come to question her…but I want to talk about us, Hans, about prom night."

Sadness and regret fill the space between them.

"Wow! Not the timid little girl I remembered…Okay." Feeling her urgency, he pauses for only a moment. "When I went to your house to pick you up that night, no one was there. At least, no one answered the door." He looks down at his hands. "I was confused and more than a little angry. I didn't want to go home and explain that I was stood up. I went to the prom. I thought I could lose myself in the crowd, hoped that maybe there was a mix-up and I would somehow find you there…." He seems to have run out of words or doesn't want to say the rest.

"I was so young and stupid, Hans. When you asked me to the prom, I decided you only did it out of pity or because it was too late to ask one of the popular girls. I never understood why you noticed me."

He opens his mouth to speak, but she continues. "We were poor. There was no money for a prom dress. I tried to make something from an old discarded party dress of Mary's. I had never cultivated friends my age, and none of my freshman class-mates were going to the prom anyway, so I had no one to talk to about it. Mary just sneered when I tried to ask her for advice.

"I thought the dress looked okay until that night. I curled my hair, trying for something different, put on Mary's makeup, and put on the dress. Mary's room had a full-length mirror. I ran down there to view myself as Cinderella.

"When Mary saw me, she started laughing. I looked and couldn't breathe. My reflection showed a little girl playing dress-up in someone else's clothes and hair and face. The shoes were wrong, and the hem of the dress wasn't even straight. I looked like a rag doll some child had tried but failed to make pretty.

"I burst into tears and that made it even worse. Mascara and blush turned my face into mud. Because there was no way to fix all that was wrong before you arrived, we turned out the lights and pretended no one was home. So, no one answered the door when you knocked. But you kept knocking, breaking my heart."

"Why didn't you tell me? I mean...afterwards?"

"I was too ashamed, and then the school year ended and you were gone...Besides, you wouldn't even make eye contact with me at school."

She looks up into his eyes and cannot look away. "I knew I had humiliated you, and everyone else knew it. Even my own classmates looked at me like I was some kind of freak. They called me a tease, a bitch...and of course, crazy. Soon it had nothing to do with the prom; it was just how everyone thought of me, how I began to see myself. It seemed like my life changed then—like I hit a wall that night, and finally crossed through, a different person—someone even I didn't like."

He looks down at his coffee. "My friends were angry because you stood me up. They started rumors. Your name began appearing with Mary's on bathroom walls above the urinals."

"Oh!"

He looks up at her again. "I should have done something. But my ego was hurt, and I didn't. I've never stopped being sorry. Exams and graduation filled the rest of the semester."

"And then Boston," she whispers.

"Yes, for an early-entry summer program."

"They wrote on walls..." Ray is still trying to process this betrayal.

Hans's misery seems to grow. "I was responsible for that, and for Mary's reputation as well."

"What?...Mary?"

"I met her when we first moved here," he says quickly, as if to get the words out before he can change his own mind. "I didn't think I would ever have the chance to tell you this. I'm glad that I finally can."

Chapter Fifty-Two

He takes a deep breath and continues, "Mary and I…'hooked up' is what the kids would say today…at a party, soon after school started. She was funny and so pretty. I was shy and hardly knew anyone there. I came late; she had already been drinking. Without even a 'hello,' Mary walked up and kissed me in front of everyone."

"Please stop, Hans. I don't want to hear this."

"I'm sorry, but I have to tell you what happened…Maybe she was drunk…but she seemed to know exactly what she was doing…At least I thought she did."

"What do you mean?"

He looks up at her, and she can see the boy again.

"She led me to a room where we had awkward, unplanned sex."

Hans had sex with Mary?

Ray shakes her head and finds her voice, saying the first inane thing that comes to mind. "Awkward?"

"We were both virgins."

Was Mary ever a virgin?

"I thought she was experienced and could teach me." In a small voice he adds, "Maybe she thought the same. But it was embarrassing, and over in less than a minute. When I apologized, she started screaming, so I got dressed and left the room…and the party."

Unable to look at his face, Ray stares at the table.

"I tried to talk to her the next week, but she ignored me and flirted with whatever boy was nearby. I started hearing locker room talk about her sexual appetite and bragging from boys who claimed to have had her. In fact, her nickname became One-Night Mary."

Ray barely hears his last words. She's too busy doing the

math in her head. Her mind recoils and then grows numb. "Hans, are you telling me that you're Allie's father?"

Fair-haired, blue-eyed, science-minded Hans fathered dark-haired, brown-eyed, musical Allie? Impossible!

"I honestly don't know. But I felt responsible for Mary's indiscriminate behavior after that night, like my inept blundering had somehow triggered it. And...yes...I might be Allie's father. I hadn't used a condom, didn't expect to need one. When I heard she was pregnant, I asked her if it could be mine. Mary just laughed in my face, and said I wasn't the man I imagined myself to be."

"Sounds like Mary—always being a smart-ass to protect her very real insecurities. She was partly right. You weren't strong enough to make her into the person she was. She probably went to the party determined to do exactly what she did—lose her virginity. And maybe she didn't get pregnant that night."

But then another thought creeps unbidden into Ray's consciousness. She tries to shove it away, but it will not leave.

What if Mary learned she was pregnant and then slept with various boys so no one would know (especially Hans) that he was the father? Maybe she'd cared for him, had purposefully sought him out to be her first. Maybe she cared too much to tie him to an unplanned baby. I remember Carla demanding to know who the father was, threatening to put him in jail. Through multiple random sex partners, Mary protected Hans.

And maybe jealousy had kept Mary from helping me become presentable for the prom.

Ray has to stop there, knowing it's too much to take in all at once. It's almost as if she never knew Mary at all.

They let silence fill the space for a while. And then another truth creeps in.

"So, is that why you started talking to me at the waterfront?" she asks. "You wanted to meet the baby that might be yours?"

"At first...but it's not why I kept coming. I loved watching the two of you, the bond between you, almost as if you were the mother, not Mary. And I wanted to tell you about me and my family so that in the future, you might share my stories with Allie—in case she *was* mine."

"Why didn't you get a paternity test?"

"Because Mary refused. And a year after Allie was born, I graduated and left for college in Boston. I wasn't mature enough to handle the complications with you and Mary. I couldn't see how you could ever care about me if you knew the truth. So, I left without saying anything.

"And then the accident happened. I didn't learn about it until weeks later, when I ran into a high school friend. I got in my car and drove straight here."

"From Boston?"

He nods, and the strain on his face is what Ray saw from her attic window so long ago.

"Your mother answered the door. I told her I might be Allie's father and asked to see her and you. She said you were gone but told me to go to the backyard. A small child with large, sad eyes came outside and hopped, skipped, and walked to the tire swing where I waited. It seemed like she remembered me. I know that's impossible. But she crawled up on my lap and leaned back against my chest. Instead of swinging, we spun, and she giggled."

"Then you got up and put her on the swing, and you pushed her."

"You were there?"

"Yes. I watched from the attic dormer window."

He lets this sink in. "So, you've been here all along, and I never knew. I just assumed you had left for college, and I thought I had done enough damage to your family, so I didn't ask where you were…thought you wouldn't want to see me anyway. But I did keep up with Allie. She went to school in Boston where I had a practice. A few years after I learned she'd returned here to teach high school band, I decided to move here. I missed the climate, the small-town atmosphere…And my wife had left me. There was nothing to keep me in Boston."

"Left you?" Ray whispers, still trying to process all that he has said.

"We had many problems. Divorce seemed like the only solution. I suppose it had never been a good marriage. Why am I telling you all this? You were always the only person I could really talk to."

"I'm sorry," she shrugs. "I mean, about the divorce."

But I'm not! I am staggered by betrayals!

"So, it was all about Mary and Allie." Ray shakes her head to clear it of the regret she knows will follow. "I was in love with you, Hans. After you left and Mary started taking me out with her, she thought it was funny that I never cared about any of the boys we met. She said the worse I treated them, the more they wanted me. She said I was the perfect wing-girl, attracting the men, then rejecting them so they turned to her."

"Ray," Hans whispers as he reaches for her hands on the table. She slides them back, folds them in her lap.

"Of course, it wasn't my looks; it was the 'don't give a damn' attitude that made them buzz around me. I wasn't interested in them because I was already in love—with you. In the end, they were happy to be handed off to Mary. After all, she was the pretty and willing one…After the wreck, everything was different. Mary was gone, and my one focus became Allie. Sorry again. Talking too much must be contagious."

His jaw is slack at these revelations. "You still don't know how lovely you are." She blushes and frowns her denial.

"Raynelle, I invited you to the prom because you were the one person I wanted to go with. I never cared for the popular cheerleader type. And Mary wasn't my type either. You were."

Ray shakes her head, still unable to accept the meaning of his words. "Why didn't you ever say anything?"

"Why didn't you? We were both still children, Raynelle. Both of us too shy and too sensitive to see the truth in our feelings, or to speak plainly of them. My memory of you kept me going through years of loss: my mother, my grandfather… every patient whose heart health went south, my wife's rejection after…

"I have been talking to the girl at the waterfront with the infant in her arms for most of my life. Those memories brought sunshine and comfort. You truly were my ray of light."

Something moves in her peripheral vision. She turns to look closer. It's a group of men or boys in windbreakers. It's almost summer and warm outside. They're hiding something. Before she can get up, they disappear into the waiting elevator. Allie is on the third floor. The lights above the elevator show it stopping at the second floor and then coming down again. The doors open, and an elderly woman emerges.

They got off on the second floor…and maybe took the stairs.

She gets up and runs, pushing all that Hans has revealed from her mind.

Chapter Fifty-Three

As if in a dream, Allie hears a flute playing an Irish ballad from the spring concert. A triangle and then light bells join the flute. The dream is rich in sensory memory. A slight tapping pulls her closer to the surface. The sound comes closer, reverberating on her bed frame, forcing her to waken, to open her eyes.

In the almost-dark room, she sees the musicians, boys from her band. No, wait! The drummer at the foot of her bed pulls back her hood and bright curls emerge.

"Katie?"

At that moment, Ray rushes into the room and almost falls to the floor in relief when she sees the unthreatening intruders. The boys acknowledge her with a nod. Their eyes seem hollowed and sad.

"Oh my," Allie whispers, tears surfacing and streaming down her face. The bed is already raised at the head so she can see them in the early morning's beginning light. The music fades and Katie drops her sticks as she rushes to the side of her teacher's bed.

"We were so worried, Ms. Nichols."

"How did you get in here? Never mind. I probably don't want to know. I'm going to be fine, Katie. What happened to your hand?" The girl slips her bruised and scraped hand behind her back. One of the boys speaks.

"We were holding a vigil for you and Marcus at the school gym, and two of Buck's friends, John Perry and Larry Green, had been drinking and started bragging to the news crew that they knew what was going down. Some plainclothes cops showed up, and they were arrested. We saw two others, the Carlson twins, head for the locker room. Some of the band had a 'come to Jesus meeting' with the jerks—which means we turned Katie loose on them."

The flautist snickered. "After that, they turned themselves in."

That leaves one truant not accounted for, Mike Harris—clever

Mike Harris.

The door opens and the guard, finally awake, clears his throat. "All right. No visitors. Outta here, now!"

"Hey dude," the flautist asks, "can't you just give us a minute?"

"I said out, DUDE! All of you, NOW!"

Ray is in the shadow of the privacy curtain, unseen by the policeman.

"Love you, Ms. Nichols." Katie whispers in Allie's ear, "Let me know what our story is because I honestly don't know what happened, and I can always just stick to that, but...for Marc's sake...I'll say whatever you want. I've avoided the cops. But they'll know whose gun was there. So, they'll question me sooner or later." She gives a meaningful look, and they're gone.

Katie rushes back in, hands the drumsticks and a small box to Allie. It's a box of putty for making a practice drumhead.

Allie stares at the sticks and putty, amazed by Katie's insight.

"You all right?" the officer asks.

"Yes," Allie responds, wiping her eyes and blowing her nose, "but please don't tell anyone I'm awake. I need some time before I have to answer questions. I'm still a little confused."

He hesitates for only a moment. "No problem. You just rest. By the way, my nephew is in your band—Jamie, the freaky kid with purple hair. Stories get around. You may have saved his life by cancelling rehearsal. We're all beholden."

Allie follows him with her eyes. When the door closes, she lifts one of the drumsticks and her lips begin to open, forming an "O."

In her mind, broken images flash by, broken faces, broken bodies—broken boys.

Chapter Fifty-Four

Mike approaches the gymnasium, with his father's gun an unaccustomed weight in his pants pocket. Two more cops have been posted at the entrance, a male and a female. The man pats down the guys as they enter, and the woman pats down the girls.

Very P.C., he thinks. *Everybody's being watched, even the cops.*

Frustration is fed by anger as he realizes he can't get in with the gun. His hand reaches in and out of his pocket—touching the cold metal, a reminder of his purpose. He turns to walk away, then turns back again—pulled like a magnet to the people who had always humiliated him.

The gym is swarming with band members. The plan was to finish what Buck and BJ started. BJ! He'd never liked Mike... and the feeling was mutual. He'd tried to make Mike feel even smaller by calling him Shrimp. The name caught on. Everyone called him Shrimp...except for Buck, who never did.

He knows this could be suicide. He planned to use his bullets on anyone near and then throw the gun down and raise his arms. He'd be arrested, go to prison with Buck. They'd be in charge there—just like at school.

He has to do something.

I can't go back to school without Buck. I would become everyone's target for what went down—even though I wasn't there when the shooting happened.

He pauses, accepts the impossibility of getting into the gym...then turns and heads to the hospital.

Chapter Fifty-Five

Allie refuses to allow her mind to dwell on yesterday. Ray covers Allie's hand holding the drumstick.

"What are you thinking, my girl?"

"I'm thinking I'm twenty-seven, not a girl anymore."

"Well, actually you're twenty-eight. It's your birthday, remember?"

She doesn't react, so Ray prattles on. "The old folks at the hospice center assure me that you'll be a girl until you're at least forty. Then you'll be a woman for the next forty years. At eighty, you might consider yourself to be getting old—or you might not."

"Hmmm…what happens after that?"

"Well, you have the remaining years to prepare others to live without you. And in ten or twenty more—whenever you've had enough—you leave."

"Just leave," Allie sighs, "on your journey to a better place. Sometimes that seems kind of inviting."

"Sometimes it does," Ray agrees.

"Umm," she groans in response. "I'm thinking I don't want to think, especially about age. Wait…Old Dog. Whatever happened to Old Dog?"

"Don't you remember? He died, Allie."

Allie smiles with regret. "Wow! You used the 'd' word…I remember. I expected him to disappear, to go to a 'better place,' like my pet turtle, the neighbor's cat, and…and Mama."

She didn't say Mary, just "Mama." That single word was so much more intimate, held so much more warmth—had been missing in both of their lives for so long.

Ray adds, "We went to the backyard and picked late azalea blooms. Do you remember?"

"Yes. And we covered Old Dog with them. When Aunt Carla woke up, I was outside on my tire swing. I heard her scream and then curse. When I went back to our room, Old Dog was gone."

"To a better place?"

"Well, that's what Aunt Carla told me, and you agreed."

"No one wanted you to suffer, Allie…Can we talk about school?"

Her response is turning to impatience. "As a teacher or as a student?"

"Student."

"I don't remember much about the early years." Impatience is turning to irritability. "I read and focused on the stories in my books, ignored the way the other kids made fun of my big eyes and called me fat and crazy. How do we survive childhood?"

She sighs, damps the anger. "School got better after I met Bernie, and better still after I joined the band. Where are you going with this, Ray? I haven't forgotten everything—just the few awful things *you* bring up."

"If you knew what you had forgotten, it wouldn't be forgotten." A feeble attempt at humor. "How do you feel, Allie? Are you in pain?"

"Mostly I'm just sore. It's bearable, and I don't want any more drugs."

"Okay. I would like to take this slower, but there are things we need to remember and talk about before the police get here. Your story needs to be right."

"Then why are we talking about my childhood?"

"I suppose that was my own agenda. It has waited twenty-four years; it can wait a little longer. We'll skip ahead." Ray lies on the covers beside Allie, using as little space as possible as she carefully begins the recent past in images that she knows will explode in Allie's mind.

"Let's start with yesterday. You were in the band room with Marc and Katie."

"I haven't forgotten yesterday, Ray. I just didn't want to

talk about it until I had to."

"Humor me, Allie. It will help us get our story straight."

She sighs and reaches over to hold Ray's hand as if she needs her cousin's strength to revisit these all-too-recent memories.

"It was the end of the school day. Marc and Katie came early to band practice…I was frantic, upset because Katie had brought a gun to school. She handed it to me. I put it on my desk. She said she wanted me to have it, thought I was in danger…She and Marc were sure Buck and BJ were planning something big."

"You wanted to alert the authorities," Ray says, encouraging more details.

"But Katie and Marc had tried that in the past and nothing came of it because there was never any evidence, only their word against Buck's and BJ's…BJ…he's a sociopath?"

"Well, I never got to know BJ, but maybe. Go on, Allie."

"Where was I?"

"They wanted you to cancel band rehearsal because they felt sure that was the scheduled target for violence."

Allie hesitates. "They were afraid there was a bomb in the band room, timed to go off during rehearsal. We looked everywhere."

Allie tenses as the images speed through her mind and take her where she doesn't want to go. The search for a bomb had been futile.

"I asked them why they were so worried. They said Katie had hacked into Buck's various social media accounts. She said there had been chatter about something happening during band rehearsal for graduation. They finally got my attention. I sent out a text to the whole band, telling them rehearsal was cancelled and would be rescheduled. And there were those Snapchat headlines about school shootings…"

"And then?"

"And then I lectured Katie about bringing a gun to school." In a smaller voice, she adds, "Even though she brought it for me."

"And then?"

"I don't remember."

"Come on, Allie."

"I don't want to remember, Ray."

Ray rises from the bed, drags a chair closer, and sits. She gently asks, "Can we talk about BJ?"

"Okay!" Allie barks. "All right!" Her speech is rapid, warding off the memory with words they already know. "The transfer, BJ, the guy whose family moved here because he was kicked out of the last school he attended…His eyes were open… blood everywhere…" She pauses, trying to find the thread of what she had been saying. When she finds them, the words spill from her mouth. "His juvenile records are sealed, but not the mouths of his former classmates. We all knew he was the worst possible influence on Buck…And, like Buck…he can turn on the charm and an innocent act that would convince the Spanish Inquisition…Maybe BJ *is* a sociopath…or a psychopath."

"Maybe he was," Ray gently adds.

"Was," she whispers and then closes that mental door and closes her eyes. Ray lets her rest a moment as she continues the thoughts they had exchanged about Buck and BJ.

"It seems that there was a magnetism between the two of them. Before BJ, Buck had simply been threats and intimidation—an internal anger, no action. BJ became his catalyst and then his enabler…It just occurred to me that maybe BJ bullied Buck."

Allie's eyes are closed. Ray carefully shakes her shoulder. "Can't escape into sleep this time. You have to remember the details, get your story straight. You know the police will be here soon and make you tell it. The words you use can either end or open a whole new world of hurt for Marc and for Buck."

"All right!" she growls and blows out a breath. "Sorry, I know you're trying to help. But you're making me change—*in one day*—a lifetime habit of reality-escape which, by the way, you actually helped create."

"*Mea culpa.* But now can we move forward?"

"Buck had changed. He lost weight, never came by, although I did try to reach out to him. BJ was always there—using up all the air in the room—preventing real contact between Buck and me. But they left my students alone…until yesterday."

Allie closes her eyes again, this time not trying to escape but instead trying to recall the images, trying to recreate the moment. "I was getting my purse and about to leave…I can't remember."

"Put it into the present. Maybe you'll remember if you re-live it."

"Thanks a lot!" She sucks in a breath and then blows it out. "Okay!…Here goes." She closes her eyes again to recreate the classroom and the moment. "'Take the gun home,' I say to Katie. 'And don't tell anyone you brought it here. That could get you into so much trouble.'

"Suddenly…" Her eyes fly open as the force of the moment she has resisted arrives and the words form. "…BJ…and then Buck…burst into the room! They're wearing hats and sunglasses, almost unrecognizable…BJ raises his arm, a pistol in his hand, and aims it at Katie…Buck follows BJ, but more slowly, pointing his weapon at Marc.

"I scream, 'STOP!' It's a surreal tableau, everyone frozen in place. They are, after all, just children. An authoritative voice makes them respond…just long enough for me to call out to Buck a phrase he hates but one that I know will get his attention…'What's wrong with you, Buck?'

"He lowers his gun and looks at me with confusion on his face, like he doesn't know how or why this is happening…BJ slices at the air with his gun and screams in frustration, 'Where is everyone?'

"Katie screams at him, 'They're gone, dickhead! We cancelled rehearsal!'

"BJ says, 'Then you'll have to do, bitch.' And he aims his gun at Katie again. I look to you, stooped down where they can't see you…and you look at my hand—at the drumstick I'm holding. Everything happens at once. I throw the stick at BJ; you yell as you leap toward Katie; he sees you, but turns the gun to me…and fires…"

Chapter Fifty-Six

"…just as Marc must have grabbed the gun from the table…" Ray guesses, as neither of them saw what happened next—only the sound of gunshots.

"BJ's bullet knocked me sideways." She stops, blinking her eyes. "What happened, Ray? Who else got hurt? Katie was here. She's okay. What happened to Marc?"

"Marc will be all right. We both missed some of the action, but not all. I covered Katie, closest person to me. Shots were fired and when I looked up, Marc was sliding down a wall, injured but conscious. Buck and BJ were both on the floor. I crawled from Katie to you."

"I do remember seeing Marc, knowing he wasn't dead," Allie gasps. "So, Marc shot them both?…Is he all right?"

"Relax. They're here, in the hospital. I've already told you Marc and Buck will both live…but not BJ. He died before the first responders got there."

For a moment, Allie can't speak as she digests what she already suspected…already knew.

"I remember you and Katie leaning over me. She was screaming. I told her to hush; she was giving me a headache. She ran to Marc," Allie pauses, reaching for details. "He seemed to be hurt but alert."

She stops there, focused on Marc. Ray keeps her mind moving. "Then you told her to bring the gun and to wipe it clean. She did and then handed it to you. But you couldn't hold it, much less pull the trigger. So, I put my finger over yours…"

"…and helped me. We shot into the wall…." She sighs, overwhelmed by the remembering.

"…to get the gunpowder residue on your hand and to maybe prove the trajectory. Why did we do that, Allie?"

"We knew Katie and Marc would get into trouble, even though it would have been self-defense. But I knew it wasn't that simple. I told Katie to get out before security got there. Wait! What about the gunpowder on Marc's hand?"

"After she called 911, Katie cleaned his hand with wet wipes." Ray has to laugh. "The girl was everywhere, doing everything.

"Allie, who knows what Buck and BJ's plan was? They had thought the band room would be full. Maybe they'd planned to shoot everyone. But with no one else there, they certainly would have killed the three of you...and me. And then, knowing they'd get caught anyway, they might have gone outside and randomly killed anyone they encountered. I don't know how much ammunition they had with them. When you threw that drumstick, it changed the whole dynamic; it drew the attention of both shooters."

"I wouldn't have thrown it if you hadn't looked at my hand...at my stick. It was almost like you willed me to throw it...BJ's dead?" she asks in a little-girl voice.

"Yes, he is."

Her eyes fill with unshed tears. "What about Buck? How badly is he hurt?"

"Head wound, not serious."

She hesitates before asking..."And Marc?"

"Shoulder wound. He's very lucky."

"Like me," she finishes.

Ray hands her a tissue and she holds it against her eyes, then blows her nose. "I don't know why my first instinct was to take the blame for the gun, but I knew that if Marc became the focus of this, he might be seen as the cause of it all. He fits the mold—an unhappy bullied kid. I used to worry that Marc, not Buck, would come to school one day with a gun and open fire on his bullies. I've always wanted to protect him from himself, like I did the first time we met—when he drew a knife on Buck and his friends."

"Actually, he did do exactly that. He and Katie brought a gun to school, and he shot his two bullies. Told by BJ's grieving father, the story could, in fact, make Marc the villain."

"Oh God," Allie wails, "BJ was awful, but he was still somebody's son."

And finally, Allie breaks down, sobbing. Ray hands her another tissue to sop up the tears and snot that now pour like an open faucet.

After a while, she blows her nose with the tissue and wipes her eyes with her sheet. "So, what do I tell the police? I didn't see what actually happened."

"Well Allie, you have a choice. You can tell them the truth, which by now is so convoluted because of the way we messed with the crime scene. They, and the press, might screw it up—or purposefully slant it.

"Or you can tell them a partial truth. Katie brought you the gun because she was afraid for you—true. BJ and Buck came in with their own guns drawn and aimed at the kids—also true. You threw the drumstick to divert their attention—true—then grabbed the gun which was on your desk. You fired the gun, and then you were hit. Can't remember if you fired again, can't remember more than flashes. So much happened at once—not true, but maybe worth a try."

Allie begins reworking the story. Her eyes brighten. "New order of events. So, I shot Buck, who had already shot Marc, and then I fired at BJ who simultaneously fired at me...It all happened so fast, officer." Her look of innocent sincerity on her red-from-crying face makes Ray choke with laughter.

"Wait! I told Katie to leave, pretend she wasn't there. How do I explain the gun?"

"It's her father's gun, Allie. You have no choice. Just say you told her to get help. And to shield her from repercussions, you also told her to stay out of the situation. Katie actually didn't see what happened because I was on top of her. As she said, she'll do whatever you ask to protect Marc. But they will grill you. Can you remember to tell it just this way, over and over?"

"Considering how good I have been at burying the truth throughout my life, I think I can replace the real story with one that will protect Marc. I just have to tell him. I think it won't matter what Buck says—if he even remembers the details with his head injury. I'll text Katie now. She's probably with Marc anyway…" Allie pauses, overwhelmed.

"Let me talk to them. The police will check your phone for messages."

"Right…God…finally I'm getting some clarity and seeing all the loopholes. But what if they're already questioning Katie?"

"They don't know about her yet. They don't really know anything except that the shooting was contained. I'm sure they know you had cancelled rehearsal. Anyone in the band would have told them that much."

And then suddenly they both release a great sigh. It's done.

The peace of the moment is interrupted by sounds from outside, the sound of music instruments being fine-tuned. They both listen and then hear the beginnings of the medley from this year's marching band competition theme. Ray rushes to the window and tries to raise it for better hearing. It won't budge, so she moves Allie's bed and the medical equipment a little closer to the window.

Allie listens and smiles through new tears. She lifts the box Katie brought her, and Ray opens it, removes the putty, and helps her spread it out to form her portable drumhead.

Ray realizes her own face is wet and searches for a tissue by the sink near the door, then collapses into a chair to listen and give up a silent prayer.

Allie takes the drumstick in her one usable hand and begins to slowly tap a pattern of sound that complements the music from outside.

Chapter Fifty-Seven

Mike Harris steps from the elevator and immediately identifies Buck's room by the cop sitting in front of it. He ducks into the hall to his right when the cop stirs, gets up, stretches, and walks down the hall to the nurses' station, probably to snag some coffee.

Mike quickly moves past a door with the name "Darby" on it and notices the name "Nichols" on the third room.

He slips into Buck's room and closes the door, then breathes a sigh of relief at the sight of his friend. Buck is the only one who ever treated him with kindness. The smaller boy has always felt protected and even enlarged by Buck's size and power. He liked the way other students shrank back against their lockers when they walked the school halls together. And now his idol looks pathetically powerless, tied to a bed, bandages over half his face.

Mike slides his hand against the gun in his pocket. He slowly wraps his fingers around it, releasing the safety and carefully sliding his index finger next to the trigger. It feels solid and heavy. He feels solid and strong. His thoughts are interrupted by movement in the bed.

Buck wakes and turns his head to see a familiar face.

"Mike, what are you doin' here?…Get me some water… and untie my hands."

Mike sets the gun down to untie Buck's restraints. "Maybe I can do this for you."

"Do what? God, my head hurts!"

"I can show all of them how wrong they've been about me—everyone who has treated me like I'm nothin'. You're goin' to prison for what happened yesterday, Buck. I can finish what you and BJ started…can go to prison with you…"

Chapter Fifty-Eight

The hall is empty and quiet when Buck steps from his room. The IV needle is still in his hand, the drip bag disconnected and hanging uselessly from its pole. The left side of his face is bandaged, forcing him to turn his head to see the numbers beside the doors. The pain of that movement elicits a gasp that no one hears.

Everyone must be at a window, listening to the band.

He motions Mike toward the elevators, wanting him gone before anyone comes out and sees.

Mike hasn't done anything except bring me a gun. He can do the time for that standing on his head. He can still have a life.

He slowly opens the door to room 314 with the name "Allie Nichols" printed beneath. The sound of the music reaches his unbandaged ear. He realizes for the first time that he never hated the band students. He just envied them.

Unwilling to risk the pain of turning his head again, he enters the room soundlessly, blind to anything on his left. So, he doesn't see the woman, Ms. Nichols's cousin, who is always with her. She's in a chair beside the opened door, unable to move for fear it might startle him, make him fire the gun already aimed at Allie.

Her bed is directly in front of him near the window, and she is a silhouette in the morning light—sitting up, tapping on something in her lap with a drumstick. Focused on the music and her students outside, she doesn't sense or hear him.

She has never heard me. Why did she pick the pervert's kid? Why not me?

He's young and injured. He should be nervous, unsure. But his hand holding the revolver is steady. There's no doubt in his mind about what he has to do. There's no other way out.

The security guard rolls past on his Segway, around the corner without seeing Buck.

"I don't know!" Buck whispers, as Allie turns and recognizes him, her drumstick frozen in the air. For a moment, he hesitates, surprised by her glasses, by the way they make her eyes look so large and her whole face so fragile—open and unprotected.

"I don't know! Do you understand?…Never mind! Scream, and I'll shoot the cop or whoever comes in. Now drop it!" he growls, gesturing at the drumstick.

The stick clatters as it hits the floor and Allie slowly lowers her hand to the covers, struggling to control her face, to drain the fear while trying to think.

"You look different," he mutters.

She glances down at her bandages and all the tubes and blinking medical equipment. "We both look different. Things happened, Buck."

"No, I mean the glasses. Not like yourself…more like a kid."

"When I was a kid," she says shakily, buying time, "other kids teased me about my large eyes. The glasses make them seem even larger. Children can be unkind, but they don't have to be. It's a choice, Buck."

In spite of the closed window, the music from the band grows louder as it reaches a crescendo. He speaks above the competing sound, confident his voice will not be heard. "Wow! I couldn't have planned this better. I could do you while the band plays on. Want to know why, MIZ BAND TEACHER?"

The music outside softens as it nears the end of the song.

"You got me suspended for beating up the pervert's kid," he hisses, lowering his voice to the level of the music. "Everything is your fault! Everyone in school watched me, waited for me to make a mistake and get kicked out for good. My dad watched me. He's your fault, too. And the cops are coming for me because of yesterday. I DON'T KNOW!!! Got no place to go but down."

Allie's eyes widen, a flicker of understanding. She finds her voice. "You're right! The police are coming. They're coming now, Buck. You haven't killed anyone. If you turn yourself in…"

"No, teach, no turnin' myself in. Not my style. And you're wrong. BJ's dead…and…"

"Yes, but that's not your fault. And Marc's alive. You didn't kill him. It's too late for BJ, but not for you."

"You don't understand…After he shot you, *I* killed BJ. I didn't want to come…I didn't want to kill anyone. But BJ made me. And now I have to finish what we started."

Grasping at a straw, she tries again to change the direction of his thoughts. "What did you mean when you said, 'I don't know'?"

Like yesterday, he pauses and for a moment lowers his gun. His lips twist as he tries to formulate an answer. "I don't know…what's…wrong…with…me…I've told you over and over, but you don't help."

Behind him, Ray can't see his eyes but she can hear the emptiness in Buck's voice as he accepts his life's end, the same emptiness she has witnessed so many times just before a terminally ill person consciously stops the tired process of living.

Ray speaks softly, not wanting to frighten him with her presence. "She's right, Buck. It's not too late. You still have a choice."

He whirls at the sound of her voice, searching for its origin, aiming his gun in her direction but slowed by the bandage covering his eye, surprised when he sees Ray.

"Buck!" Allie calls.

His head jerks back, but the putty drumhead is already airborne, like a frisbee or raw pizza dough. He ducks and it hits the far wall. Buck whirls again at a sound in the doorway, gasping at the pain all the turning causes him.

A voice cries out, "STOP, Buck…please!"

Before he can process the words or the voice, Buck aims blindly at the doorway and fires. There's a moment's pause for recognition. He cries out again, this time in horror, then turns the gun to his own head, and fires for the second time. His body flies backward onto Allie's bed as two more bullets from the Segway cop's gun enter the already-dead boy.

Chapter Fifty-Nine

A series of isolated sounds: the bullets; Buck's head and chest exploding; Allie's scream; feet running; voices, some timid and some authoritative; doors slamming. From the hall comes the sound of a loudspeaker: "Code Black, Code Black."

Allie reaches for Buck, his lifeless body draped across her legs.

It's as if someone pushed the replay button from yesterday. Another room momentarily sweetened by music now holds echoes of violence with almost the same actors—as if yesterday was merely a dress rehearsal for today, the grand opening.

The room is suddenly filled with the security guard and medical personnel. One of them kneels beside the body in the doorway, calls out orders to her support team, then moves into the room to assess the two other patients. Buck and Allie are already surrounded. By her sobbing and her cries of anguish, Ray knows Allie is unhurt, at least physically.

To her surprise, she can feel her muscles as she moves… feel a three-dimensionality she hasn't known in years, as if she's no longer a non-person, a ghost to everyone but her Allie—the screaming woman.

Ray can't look at Buck, knowing what she would see—the destroyed face in her nightmare. The woman in the doorway has already been moved to a gurney and is being rolled down the hall. The finally alert cop has returned and steps over the empty Segway and past Ray. Allie muffles her ongoing screams with a pillow.

Ray staggers, almost crumples from the realization of all that has happened and all that might have happened—again. For a moment she knows exactly how Allie feels, as if she were inside her, feeling it with her, crying and screaming with her.

She can see Frank in front of Marc's closed door in what might have been a last attempt to protect him. In the room where Buck had been, Ray sees his cloth restraints on the floor. They hadn't used handcuffs—hadn't thought them necessary.

The hospital is on lockdown. They may find Mike, who probably brought the gun and released Buck. She describes Mike Harris to the hospital security cop.

Unable to bear the crowd and the sounds, and knowing she can't help Allie while so much is happening literally on top of her, Ray flees the crowded hall and finds Hans as he turns the corner, a look of terror on his face.

"She's all right," Ray chokes. "A boy is dead, but Allie's no longer in danger. She's surrounded by nurses and police. I can't help her." She falters. "Maybe I never could."

His tense face caves inwards with relief as he reaches for her. She shakes her head.

If he holds me, I'll collapse, shatter into a million pieces.

He understands and, instead of an embrace, he takes her hand.

Chapter Sixty

I have waited a lifetime for this, for the way my hand feels in his as we walk down the hall. I erase everything else that has just happened, walk away from disaster into oblivion, away from the years without him. It is enough, this warmth, this awareness only of his hand, its bones and blood and nerves pulsing against my own...Why is Hans limping?

A door opens and closes; a lock is turned. In the dark, he lifts her fingers to his lips, moist and soft. She knows instantly that what has already overwhelmed and awakened her senses is not enough. She now desperately needs to be held, needs to blot out the images of yesterday and this morning—all the fear and anger and violence, all the loss.

I can't bear the pain. So, I shut it down. I shut down every-thing but the moment. I have no choice. Hans is kissing me.

She hasn't felt the intimacy and pleasure of a kiss in years. Slowly, she responds, and then fiercely—with all the need that has been building since she first saw him this strange morning of reliving the past and surviving the present. He hesitates at first, unsure. But her hungry lips encourage his hands as they move up her arms, press softly against her bare back, then slide the straps of her sundress over her shoulders and down, his mouth following the descending cloth with tender strokes and kisses.

Desire, more intense than anything she has known, fills her body and erases all doubt—leaving only the need to absorb, to connect, to feel. He picks her up and carries her to a place as soft and yielding...as she is.

Somewhere in this space of timelessness, she finds that touching is as pleasurable as being touched. Soft moans in her ear trigger responses her body has never known as they find their rhythm and explore the magic of skin on skin.

Afterwards, she lies in his arms while the room slowly brightens with the growing intensity of the morning sun. They are on a hospital bed but not in a patient room. There are framed certificates on the wall and a desk by the window. The desk holds files and prescription bottles.

Right. He's a doctor.

"Is this your office?" she asks, immediately embarrassed by the dumb question.

"Sort of. It's temporarily my space."

"Why do you have a bed in your temporary office?"

"Sometimes I sleep here...and I take naps."

Babies and old people take naps...and sick people. Shut up, stupid intuition! Oh God, he's sick. He's sick! The prescription bottles...they're his.

They are on their sides, facing each other. At this moment, with his glasses gone, his hair tousled, and his cheeks still pink from the exertion of passion, Hans looks like the young boy on the waterfront. He gently strokes her face.

"I still can't believe it's you, much less that you're finally here in my arms and naked as the day you were born...When I first saw you, I thought fate was finally being kind. For just a moment, I didn't realize you would be here because of Allie, not me."

"I knew you were back but had avoided you," she sighs, "for both our sakes. I didn't want you to see and know me. You're a successful doctor, and I'm a professional student...been sitting in on or taking college classes for over twenty years. It's as if I've been in limbo or a self-inflicted purgatory, looking for answers or some kind of direction.

"But then when you did see me, and we both sort of bared our souls—acknowledged our past mistakes, I hoped it was a reconnection, a new and better beginning...It's not that simple, is it?...It's not a beginning."

Hans doesn't respond. So, she adds, "It's okay. You don't have to talk about it."

Obviously relieved that she knows his final truth, he slips past her pain and sympathy, rolling onto his back and pulling her on top of him.

"Tell me about the life you and Allie shared before she went to college in Boston. I was there, aware of her presence, aware of her successes in university and watching her evolve from a girl to a woman. She was amazing—*is* amazing."

"You watched over her when I couldn't?" Ray manages in a hoarse whisper, still dealing with the suspicion he has just confirmed.

He's sick, really sick…

"In a way. If you promise not to tell her, I'll let you in on a secret, something I've never told anyone."

She's listening, but her mind keeps wanting to shut down, to resist what she is powerless to change. Nevertheless, she whispers, "Promise."

"The anonymous scholarship that paid her out-of-state tuition at Boston U. was one I created. I'm not boasting. I did it as much for myself as for her. I wanted to see her, and I wanted to help with her education."

"Why anonymous? Why didn't you tell her?"

"Afraid of rejection, I guess. That seems to have been a pattern in my life."

"Was that because of me, because of the prom?"

He hesitates, looking beyond her, clearly considering that possibility. "No, I've always avoided confrontation. That's why I delayed asking you out when we were kids—afraid of Mary and her reaction."

I have so little experience with men, so little knowledge. He isn't just frail; he is fragile, easily hurt, easily frightened—always has been. But he has the courage to let me see that.

She lightly kisses his lips and then lays her head on his chest.

"When she was young," he continues, "I was a student with no money, no way to help my own daughter. As soon as possible, I began a secret fund for her, known only to Carla."

"Why secret?" Then Ray laughs with delight. "You must have been Carla's sugar daddy—suddenly all of that makes sense!"

"I was planning to tell Allie everything when I first moved here, but then I got a diagnosis about symptoms I'd been trying to ignore. I didn't want to introduce myself and say goodbye in the same breath. I needed to adjust to the prognosis myself."

"Tell me, please?"

"It's ALS, amyotrophic lateral sclerosis, commonly called Lou Gehrig's Disease...I'm still in the early stage."

Ray doesn't ask about the prognosis. She has seen ALS at the hospice center. She knows.

Hans clears his throat and continues. "Now I believe that she needs to hear it all from me. And I'll turn the fund over to her to use as she wishes. Anyway, I thought you were supposed to be telling me about you and Allie, all the years I missed."

"I think there's more to the secrecy of the fund than your fear of rejection."

After a moment, he sighs, "All right. It doesn't seem like the time or place to be discussing Sharyl, but I would have told you sooner or later. My ex-wife was miserably unhappy after years of trying and failing to conceive. She wanted to blame me. If she had known I had maybe fathered a child with someone else, and was providing that child with financial support, it would have been the straw that destroyed her as well as our marriage. The fund had to be a secret."

"So, you've had no other children?"

"None that lived...With the help of in vitro fertilization, she carried one baby almost to term. That loss so devastated her that she believed she had to change her life. It sounds terrible, but after she left, I was almost relieved."

Ray touches his face and gently turns it toward her. "I'm sorry, Hans, sorry for everything. Do you still love her...your wife?"

"I don't think I ever loved her, not really. There was always the memory of a girl and a baby in the way."

He tucks her hair behind her ear and lightly kisses her cheek. "I can barely believe it. After all these years, how is it that you're still here?"

Setting aside what she cannot change, she answers the question she's been asking herself more often lately. "I'm not sure. I thought it was for Allie. But she no longer needs me. Maybe I'm the one who's needed her. She's ready to face the past and all her present realities, including you. I hope she makes good choices."

"I'm sure some will be good and some not so much. That's the way it is with us mortals. It's what makes life interesting."

"Has awareness of your mortality made you a philosopher?"

"Maybe, but not a prophet. I have to ask. Is what just happened a once in my lifetime thing? Or can I touch you again? And by the way, now that I've found you, please don't leave me."

That's the second time I've heard those words today. And after all, he's the one who'll be leaving.

"You've never stopped touching me," she whispers as she rolls off of his chest and he slides over her.

She tucks the knowledge of his illness into a remote place in her heart, temporarily forgotten while his lips make a trail of kisses from her eyes down to her navel. She runs her fingers through his hair and down his back, gasping at tremors of joy and anticipation.

Chapter Sixty-One

In the hospital corridor, Ray's smile is so bright she expects it to power up the subdued lighting. She is actually surprised that no one notices. But it's a blinking light, like a short-circuited lamp.

How can I feel so sad and so happy at the same time? Oh, dear God—ALS...

A cleanup crew and a team of police are working the crime scene in Allie's old room. Ray finds her three doors away, talking on her phone. She wears a clean gown and looks haggard...but perhaps in control.

Clarity. That's what she's found, and it's what will help her deal with all that has happened.

Allie gives Ray an angry, withering look.

How long have I been gone?

"I'm glad you called, Bernie...Well, it wasn't like the other school shootings, thank God. One of the shooters died yesterday." In a broken voice, she adds, "The other one died today. I really don't want to talk about it...I miss you too. Yes, Ray's here, and don't start on her! I couldn't have survived this without her!" She grabs a tissue, then puts her phone on speaker, turning up the volume and laying it down to wipe her eyes and blow her nose. Ray hears his words too clearly.

"Sorry, Allie, I had just hoped you'd grown out of your need for Ray. I'm really bummed I can't be with you right now." Bernie's distant voice sounds sincere, but Allie hears something else—another kind of distance. After what has happened, why isn't he here or on his way?

"We have a performance tonight and travel to Denver tomorrow," he continues. "I wish you could meet me there. All my old college buddies are throwing a party after the show."

"It sounds like fun," she whispers, and the disappointment mixed with acceptance is so obvious, it seems impossible that Bernie can't hear it.

"School is almost out for you, isn't it?" he asks. "Why don't we meet at one of my performances this summer? You're my best friend, Allie. I need to see you and to know you're okay."

Allie's smile quavers but she contains the tears, holding them back until she can end the call. "I'll be all right, but my summer schedule is pretty full now. I'll email you. The nurse is here, and I have to hang up." She does.

"Nurse Raynelle, reporting for duty," Ray chirps, trying to bring a smile. It doesn't work. She sits in the chair by the bed.

"I guess that was what I needed," Allie whispers, blowing her nose again. She takes a deep breath. "I've been holding on to something that doesn't really exist. Never did.

"I already told a police lieutenant that Buck confessed to shooting BJ, which probably saved the rest of us. He'll be back to talk about yesterday. I was so emotional, he decided to give me some time while he writes up the report about today, about Buck and his mother."

"Wait! What? His mother?"

"I forgot you wouldn't know her. She'd just arrived, must have found his room empty and then saw him in mine."

"The woman in the doorway was his mother?"

He shot his mother! No wonder he turned the gun on himself! No! I'm sure he would have done that anyway.

Allie sighs, and Ray feels the emptiness in that sound, a deep hollow that is slowly filling with anger but emerges as sarcasm. "Has he gone to a 'better place,' Ray?"

For a moment she glares at her cousin. "I've lost Bernie, or my stupid idea of him. I've lost Buck…" Her mouth remains open as the realization that Buck meant more to her than she'd understood. He was the child she couldn't save. He mattered.

"His mother is alive, by the way. Luckily, his aim was impaired by the bandages."

"Allie, I don't think he would have hurt you, but I also don't think we could have saved him from himself. You know that many teens have tunnel vision. He couldn't see a way out."

Allie is silent for minutes.

"I'm not like your old lady friends, Ray. I don't want to be a girl until I'm forty. You've protected me far too long. You do need to get your own life! I meant it when I said it before the shooting. I can take care of myself! I WANT to take care of myself!"

"Okay! I'll move out!" For a moment they both look stunned. "Actually, I was trying to figure out how to tell you that I've been invited to live somewhere else."

"Somewhere else?"

"Yeah...on a boat, a beautiful wooden sailboat."

Chapter Sixty-Two

At that moment, there's a knock on the door. It opens. Marc is wheeled in by his mother, Miriam Darby. Frank follows, pulling Marc's IV stand. Their faces are drawn but clear-eyed. Miriam is stoic as always, but there's a crack in her plastic mask of serenity. And Marc just looks exhausted.

When his eyes meet Allie's, they fill. He blinks the tears away and looks down. "I'm so sorry, Ms. Nichols. This was all my fault." Her anger at Ray collapses, replaced by empathy for Marc.

"None of this was your fault. If you and Katie had not come to me and insisted that we cancel rehearsal, there's no telling how many students might be dead or injured." She looks at him intently, willing him to understand. "And if Katie hadn't brought me the gun, we would probably all be dead."

After a moment, his eyes still downcast, he says, "The police have already questioned me. I saw Buck shoot BJ. I was already reaching for the gun on your desk. If I had let it be, or if we hadn't brought it, maybe he would have just left."

"He wasn't in control, Marc. He might have just killed all of us and then himself."

"Anyway, the police said my story didn't match yours."

Allie almost laughs and then checks herself. "Actually, they haven't heard my story about yesterday yet. Maybe they were just testing you to see if you were lying. I didn't know, until Buck told me, that he shot BJ after BJ shot me. I don't even know what happened next."

Marc looks at his father for approval, before adding, "BJ acted like he was high on something. Probably had to do that to get his nerve up. After Buck shot BJ, we shot each other at the same time. I've never fired a gun before…"

"If BJ or both of them were on something, it will show up in the autopsies. I think he had been bullying Buck all this time, goading him into more and more violent behavior. I believe Buck wanted out and he had been asking me for help, but

I didn't hear him...Anyway, I guess we can tell the truth about what happened. You're a hero, Marc."

Marc sighs. "No, I'm not. I don't think Buck would have shot me. We shouldn't have brought the gun."

Frank clears his throat. He speaks softly but with grim determination. "Most people would not see Marc as a hero. They would see him as my son—the son of a criminal. He would be condemned as a part of the shooting—maybe even prosecuted. Please stick to your version—or at least Marc's involvement in your version. Keep his name out except as a victim."

Allie takes a moment to think through what Frank has just asked. "I understand. So, BJ shot me; then Buck shot him; then I shot Buck. Don't think they'll believe that even though we tried to make it plausible. Buck's mother was aware of his problems. She will not try to blame you, Marc. If you're all right with it, I think we can go with the truth."

He nods. "Thank you. I'm not a good liar."

Allie's hand trembles as she lifts it toward Marc. His mother wipes tears from her face and pushes the wheelchair closer. He takes his teacher's hand with both of his.

"Dad saw Buck's mother go to your room."

"She tried to stop him this morning," Allie whispers. "They tell me she'll be all right."

After a moment, Marc releases her hand. "I think he wanted to die."

Ray timidly interjects, "How do you feel about that?"

"Sad. I just feel sad...and I know it sounds terrible, but I also feel relieved...Maybe BJ and Buck are at peace now." He sighs and shakes his head. "Didn't think I would ever feel sympathy for either of them."

Frank hands Miriam a handkerchief, and she blows her nose, then straightens and regains her usual composure. "Thank you, Ms. Nichols. We need to go back to your room, Marcus." She almost smiles at Allie. "They're releasing him today."

Frank adds with pride, "The school has already said he

could leave for the summer. His grades are good. They're excusing him from exams. He'll be a senior next year."

"I can always use a volunteer dad's help with the band," Allie offers.

Frank's lips raise in a crooked smile. "I don't think that's allowed," he says, a reminder that his imprisonment has never ended. He cannot be around children other than his son. "Unless I work on scenery for the competition—in the summer or after school hours, of course."

"We can make that happen."

After they leave, Ray sits on the bed beside Allie. "Marc will be all right. I think Frank will be, too. He accepts his limitations."

"I hope so…I'm sorry, Ray, for the way I spoke earlier."

"That's twice you've apologized for the same thing. That may mean that you meant it, and I have to agree with you."

Chapter Sixty-Three

"There are still some things I have to tell you, and some of it's good. It needs to be said because, if I haven't learned anything else in the last twenty-four hours, I have learned that life is temporary and unpredictable. We can't wait to put things right.

"First of all, I have news that I hope you will be glad for."

"Does it have anything to do with a sailboat?"

"Don't get ahead of me. Second, I have no doubt Bernie loves you. But maybe…"

"He loves his music and himself more," she finishes for Ray. "If I had been willing to be a lifelong groupie, it might have worked for us. Many women have done that. I can't."

"Of course you can't."

"But most important," Ray continues, "I need to straighten out a misconception—pretty long overdue. We can call it a confession."

Allie looks at her cousin with those big brown eyes as if she's waiting for her to say she spilled the milk and didn't clean it up, and now it's making the whole kitchen smell sour—something inconsequential compared to everything else that has happened.

But it isn't inconsequential, and Ray has to explain so Allie can blame her instead of herself when she one day remembers the crash and what really caused it.

"The car crash, before the other car hit us…do you remember what happened?"

"No, but I guess I will," Allie responds sarcastically.

"The windows were down," Ray prompts. "It was a beautiful day and we were singing with the radio."

With an exaggerated sigh, Allie closes her eyes to blot out the present and once again visit the past. As if in a hypnotic state, she immediately begins to relive details she had long ago forgotten. "I'm pretend-directing the music with my toy drumstick."

Her hands move in 4:4 time. She pauses. A frown slowly forms.

"That's good. Go on."

"Hush! You and Mary get into an argument. You yell at each other, and you turn the radio off. I'm angry because it isn't fun anymore. It's my birthday. I scream, and Mary turns the radio back on, but you turn it off again. You fight over the stupid radio and I...I...throw the toy drumstick at you...But it hits Mary. The car suddenly stops! I guess she hit the brakes because I threw the stick and...and that's all I remember." She slowly opens her eyes, her frown deepening.

"You know what happened next, Allie."

She covers her eyes with her hands as if trying to blot out the terrifying images. She whispers, "That's when the other car hit us."

Her eyes fly open. "Oh my God! It was my fault! If she hadn't hit the brakes, he wouldn't have hit us. He would have just gone into the field on the other side of the road...I killed my mother!"

"Allie! You didn't kill anyone. You were four. It was your birthday, and we ignored you. Any child would have protested. The fault was ours."

Allie looks at Ray in confusion and disbelief, unable to let go of the memory of throwing her drumstick and the life-ending, life-changing crash that followed.

"Before we left the house, I'd found wine in Carla's closet, and Mary drank most of it. But I foolishly let her drive and then fought with her over something so trivial I don't even remember what it was. We were the adults and should've known better.

"Many witnesses saw the other car cross the lanes and hit us. No one noticed we were stopped because it had just that moment happened. It was almost simultaneous. If she hadn't hit the brakes, he would have hit the back of our car instead of the front. You would have died instead of Mary...I'm sorry...I needed you to know all the truth because I knew you would blame yourself if you remembered when I wasn't here to explain. It was our fault."

"Why wouldn't you be here? I'm sorry I told you to...to get a life." They both smile self-consciously. "I didn't mean it. Please don't leave. I'll always need you."

"And I'll always be here when you need me. But it is time for me to get a life of my own, Stick." She laughs. "I like that name."

Allie shakes her head. "I've been throwing my drumstick again lately—to get someone's attention—or to redirect it." She pauses and they look at each other. Their eyes widen and their mouths open in realization.

"You saw the other car coming." Ray whispers. "You threw the drumstick to..."

"...to get your attention. I remember. I did see it, but I couldn't say the words fast enough; I just screamed and threw the stick...Raynelle, I remember!"

"...and Mary hit the brakes instead of accelerating. If Mary and I had not been arguing, she might have seen the other car and avoided it. She was a good driver. You wouldn't have had to throw the stick; no one would have died."

Silence as they both absorb the truth, the real events of that day, the day that has haunted Ray for twenty-four years. Allie finds a tissue and wipes at her eyes. Her face evolves from anguish to resignation.

"On the other hand," she whispers, "if none of that had happened, Aunt Carla might still be a drunk; Mama might have died from AIDS or something else in her downward spiral; I might not have become a music teacher; you would've finished high school, gone to college and maybe never come home again; we would not have had all these years together."

"And you might not have saved Marc and Katie. BJ and Buck might still be alive—or not. Allie, it is what it is. You have done the very best you could." Ray takes a deep breath and slowly blows it out.

"I'm not quite finished. I have more to tell you."

"More? Oh, dear God, I don't want to hear more!"

"I understand," Ray clears her throat "but, I may have

found your biological father." Allie doesn't react or respond. In the last day, she's had enough surprises for a lifetime. She is super-saturated with shock, beyond overload, ready to crystalize. But she waits for Ray to go on.

"He's a doctor in this hospital." Allie still doesn't speak. "He plans to tell you soon, maybe even today. When he does, be kind. In his own way, he has watched over you for all of your life. But I'll let him tell you his story."

"Am I now supposed to remember something about him? It's too much, Ray. A father is more than I can think about. And if he's here, in Washington, in this hospital, why is he just getting around to telling me?"

"It's a very long story, and he's only recently moved back. Things are never as simple as you might want them to be, and people are never perfect.

"Carla and I got in the habit of trying to shield you from negative realities. We were wrong. We learn from our tragedies as well as our victories. You can get through everything that's happened. And you can do it on your own. In fact, you can do it better without me. You really don't need me anymore."

Allie frowns and her eyes fill again. She sighs. "I knew this time would come...even wondered why you hung around so long. But why now?"

"Because if things just went back to normal, I might not gather the courage to change them. It's time."

"I'll miss you," she whispers, and her tears spill. "Where will you go? Can't you at least wait until I'm well again?"

"I don't know where I'll go, but I'm not leaving any time soon. I have some unfinished business of my own with your father. Yep, another story." She sits beside her beloved cousin on the bed and holds her for a long time. Allie is physically and emotionally exhausted, her mind as well as her body wounded. And Ray can't let her go until her breathing becomes even, until she's asleep.

Chapter Sixty-Four

Hans is in his office, still napping, in an almost fetal position. Ray curls against his back and kisses his neck. He smiles and sighs but doesn't wake. In her head, a prayer forms—a prayer of thanksgiving, of supplication, of acceptance. A whisper, a word, a shake, but he still doesn't respond. Lying there without his touch or his blue eyes saying too much, a moment of objectivity finds her.

She had shaped her memories of Hans into a perfect dream and held on to it, turning away all other lesser men. She knows that he isn't her dream; he isn't perfect. He has made as many poor choices as the rest of humanity. But he shared those weaknesses and accepts hers.

"I can and will love you," she whispers, "for as long as we have." And then she too finally sleeps, unaware that his eyes open and he smiles.

Chapter Sixty-Five

In a chair pulled next to her bed, a police detective takes notes while Allie responds to his questions. She retells the story of yesterday in her band room. His responses sound skeptical. She sounds tired, complaining that she already answered these same questions for another policeman.

"So, the boy, Marcus Darby, shot Buck Bailey?"

"I assume so. I didn't see it."

"Do you know who shot first?" he asks.

"BJ shot me first. Before that, Marc and Katie came to warn me…"

"And they brought a gun."

"Katie brought it, to protect me. It was on my desk. And if she hadn't brought it, there might have been dozens more wounded or dead. I was on the floor, don't know who fired first, Marc or Buck. Since they were both hit, I would guess simultaneous."

"All right," he says, "God knows I'd rather credit a student for defending his teacher than any other scenario that might come out of this. Wish you hadn't mucked up the crime scene to make it look like you did the shooting. Don't leave your teaching job to become a cop."

"Sorry. Guess I wasn't thinking straight. Loss of blood, and all that…"

"Right!" Then he asks her the same questions again about this morning, about Buck. She answers wearily, and he hands her tissues as the tears begin.

"Well," he mutters, "you sure seem to have a good throwing arm."

"You have no idea."

The officer closes his notebook and looks at Allie again and says softly, "You don't remember me, do you?" Then he laughs a little ruefully. "Why would you? You were only four and your life had just nearly ended. It had certainly changed."

"What?"

"Happy birthday, by the way. Quite a coincidence, we meet again on your birthday."

"What?" she repeats.

"I was fifteen, on a ride-along with my dad—also a cop—when we saw the accident and stopped. I picked you up a few feet away from the wreck. Dad told me to take you across the road, a safe distance from the fire."

"I do remember someone holding me."

"I also heard later that you had a tough time adjusting to your losses. It's a small town," he adds in apology.

"You heard I was crazy—danced down the street, talked to dead people, codependent on my cousin. And of course, she's even weirder."

He was silent for a few moments. "Actually, it's not a co-incidence. I asked for this assignment because I wanted to see you and know that you'll be all right. You know you're very important to the school and the town…You also know, don't you…your mother…"

Before he can speak the words, Allie does.

"Yes, I know. Mama and the other driver, Eric Masters—they both died that day…But Mama was with me for a while, when I needed her, and I only talked to Mr. Masters a few times.

"And Raynelle, my cousin, has always been with me. And she isn't an alter ego or an imaginary friend. Even though people never seem to notice her, and she tries to make herself invisible, actually acts like a ghost. She may be a flake, but she's real and alive. That I'm sure of."

As he rises, Detective Edwards takes Allie's hand. "Stick to your story about the shootings, and you don't need to mention seeing dead people."

Exiting, he adds, "By the way, we got the kid who brought the gun to Buck."

"Mike Harris?"

"Yep."

A short time later, a doctor enters Allie's room, crosses to the chair beside her bed and sits. She looks up and studies his face.

"Do I know you?" she asks. And then a slow smile begins. "In my backyard…on my tire swing."

Chapter Sixty-Six

Ray takes her time as she walks home to pick up photos of Allie's childhood for Hans to see. At the tall yellow Victorian, Will is stooped, weeding his garden. His cell rings and he stands to answer, rubbing the hip that bothers him, the one that needs to be replaced.

"Alabama Nichols," he laughs, "I am so glad to hear your voice. They wouldn't let us see you. Carla and Abe are on their way home. Ranny is out shopping for ingredients to make casseroles for you and Raynelle." He pauses and stretches, his back to Ray. "You mean for good?…I'm sorry, Allie, but I'm also glad—for her and for you. You'll be okay on your own. We'll talk when you get home."

Ah, Will! You always know the right things to say. And we'll both need lots of talks with you.

On the opposite side of the street, Marc and his parents drive up.

Wow! Shoot and release. People spend almost no time in the hospital anymore. Safer, apparently.

Allie will make sure the world knows that his and Katie's insistence on cancelling rehearsal saved untold numbers of students. Although, like Marc said, if Katie hadn't brought the gun, Buck might have walked away after he shot BJ. Maybe BJ was always his target. That's an "if" they will both have to live with.

Another car drives past and slows.

It's Carla and Abe. They must've found an earlier flight. Good for them!

They park on the side street, not bothering to pull into the driveway.

They must be stopping for clothes for Allie. So, she's also being released—coming home.

Pick something with an elastic waist, easy to pull on—and a sleeveless loose top with buttons, not one she has to pull over her head.

Ray enters the front gate and walks around the opposite

side to the backyard, not wanting to slow their purpose. She sits in the old tire swing, remembering the countless days she—and then Allie—had played out there. She remembered Hans coming here after the crash. Something inside her aches.

She searches the ground knowing that after all the years, Mary's ashes have either blown away or become a permanent part of this land's DNA. A brown pelican flies over, heading for the waterfront and lunch. Her eyes follow him, momentarily wishing that she too could fly away, end all the leaving.

But, uppermost in her thoughts is not the present but the discovery Allie made today when she remembered throwing her toy drumstick. The crash had not been her fault—even though the stick made Mary hit the brakes. It wasn't Mary's fault either, just a natural reaction. And now she remembers what they were arguing over. Mary was tired of Ray mooning over Hans. She said he wasn't worth her time and that he had ruined both their reputations. Ray had argued back, furious at her accusations.

So maybe, deep down, I suspected the truth all along.

She slowly realizes it no longer matters who was at fault for the crash, as long as Allie doesn't blame herself. It's too large a burden for anyone. The events that sculpted their lives happened. They can't un-happen. And with that acceptance, a sense of well-being floods over her. Ray hears a hiss, like the sound of air escaping a purple balloon, the sound of guilt leaving, replaced by forgiveness.

It occurs to her then that Carla's secret smile has been gone for a long time.

And now I know her secret.

When Hans visited after the crash, he told Carla that he might be Allie's father and that he would send money as soon as he could. She knew Mary and Ray had both been fools for love, had both cared for the same boy. She hadn't known what to do with those secrets, so she had just smiled.

Was it her negativity or kindness that kept her from telling me? Does it matter? Surely, if I can forgive myself...

The screen door opens and Carla comes out, dragging a

backpack. She walks around the yard, stopping at the knockout roses to touch a soft petal. Then she sits on the low wall of ballast rocks and stares at the ground. Knowing this is a private moment for her, Ray leaves the swing, but then Carla calls her name. She stops in surprise and turns.

"What, Mama?" she asks without hesitation. Her lips part and curve in a tentative smile, as she hears the word that she didn't even know she had missed.

"Oh, Raynelle," Carla sighs, as she looks at her daughter and finally, for what seems like the first time in years, makes eye contact, "how I've missed you...I thought about you as well as Allie all the way home...I was a terrible mother to you, but I think I've been a better mother to her. She's been my redemption, she and Abe...Can't you and I...can we...?"

Unable to move, Ray wants desperately to run to her and embrace the woman who for so long she'd considered to be her nemesis, a rejecter of her own child.

For how long can we hold on to anger and disappointment? When do we let go and move forward?

But it's too much too soon. Carla also seems frozen, unable to finish her question or to move. After a moment, Ray whispers, "Go get our girl." Carla straightens, lifts the backpack to her shoulder, smiles a nod, then turns and walks away.

I love you too, Mama. Or at least I want to.

After the car is gone, forgetting the photos, Ray begins her walk to her new home.

Since seventeen, I have lived on the fringe of reality, existing only for Allie. Well, maybe not just for her. There were the newly born, the sick children, and the elderly about to die...oh yes, and dogs. I was gifted a lifetime of friendships, however brief. Finally, this state of semi-being will end.

As she nears the waterfront, she's more aware of the beautiful day. The sky is a clear Carolina blue, marred only by the white linear trail of a jet in flight. A mourning dove coos and two squirrels make harmonious chatter. A dog barks. Nature's elements and principles of design. A new day and a new song begin.

She feels like the man who walked out of his cave and saw the world's amazing reality for the first time. But she doesn't think Plato ever talked about what the man heard. She wonders if he heard music — as she does, skipping and twirling all the way to the waterfront, to a wooden sailboat.

Chapter Sixty-Seven

Late summer

The breeze picks up, and the water turns choppy. *Ray of Light* cuts through it with ease. She heels and picks up speed as the wind increases and the river broadens.

Ray stands at the wheel on this home away from home where she has spent precious months with Hans. He waits for her at the boat slip, supported by a walker with a seat for when he's too tired to stand, which has become most of the time. His legs and sometimes his hands are failing him. The ALS has picked up speed.

Hans had taken her out many times, at first for pleasure, but then to learn, to prepare for today. For the last weeks, she has done the work of sailing while he sat beside her at the wheel for moral support and an occasional teaching moment.

Today, he wants Ray to experience the same joy he felt when he first sailed solo—the awe and the sense of control along with giving up control. He said the water has much more power than the boat. It is the sailor's task to navigate that power, not to govern it. Now he gives up control of his body.

Hans resigned from the hospital to provide precious time for Allie to get to know him while she healed both physically and emotionally.

Ray is still amazed that she and her mother have found their peace. They aren't girlfriends; they will never share a bond like she's had with Allie. But they're good.

Looking up at the changing clouds, she realizes she no longer thinks of God as a he, she, or it, because that falls into the "God is made in our image" attitude.

Maybe God is formless, the culmination of all that is good. Or perhaps God simply is.

The exhilaration she feels is so unexpected. But her concern for the man waiting for her makes her turn the boat.

A storm, also unexpected and unpredicted, makes bringing *Ray of Light* back into the slip less than exhilarating. She has already brought in the sails and turned on the motor. Her first attempt is thwarted by waves pushing the boat sideways just before she enters the slip. After several attempts, she adjusts the entry, compensating for the wind and manages to fit between the piers at her slip. Hans cheers as she stows everything that needs it and rigs her ropes for foul weather. He has already called Allie to ask if they can sleep at the house instead of on a rocking boat.

Ray looks from the dock to the boardwalk where Hans is now waiting for her. His sandy hair needs cutting and blows around his eyes, reminding her of the first time she saw him. The rain will begin at any moment, so she grabs her gear and runs to help him into the car.

Tonight, because the stairs have become difficult for Hans, they make up a daybed downstairs in what was once the parlor.

"It's been a perfect day," he whispers as he carefully lies down. "I'm so proud of you."

"You're a good teacher."

They snuggle in this single bed, and she is reminded of their first time together in his hospital office. She is still overwhelmed by the feel of skin on skin, even if it is just her lips against his neck. She holds her grief in check and whispers, "Good night, my love."

Chapter Sixty-Eight

Early fall

Allie puts aside the final music for this year's marching band competition. It has kept her mind busy for the past few weeks since Hans died in his sleep from a brain aneurysm.

Ray spent those same days on the water, sailing *Ray of Light* and learning to let go. She had expected to have more time with him, but their last day and evening together was the first solo trip that ended in a storm.

It's a new school year, and as always, Allie anticipates the beginning of classes with energy and enthusiasm. She has asked Katie to be her band assistant, and will be giving her every opportunity to decide if teaching music is what she really wants to do. Marc, to her surprise, wants to study law and keep music a part of his life but not his career.

Ray is now rarely at the house, never at the band room, and no longer an employee of the hospice center. She lives on the boat and drives to Greenville every day to the university, finally working on a degree. They are all healing.

Ray told Allie that when she closes her eyes, she sees Hans's face, not the beautiful, perfect boy she first met by the river, but the fallible, loving man he became.

Allie doesn't tell her that when she closes her eyes, she sees Buck. There are no bandages on his face, no gun in his hand. He is always looking at her from a distance—across the cafeteria or the gymnasium—and he is smiling.

Allie puts the folder of music into a file and crosses the band room to sit at her drums. She picks up her sticks and for only a moment holds them against her face while memories pass without pain. She lowers one stick, then the other, and begins a slow beat as her students enter and find their seats. She increases the tempo, then improvises, searching—until she loses herself and finds her escape, her freedom, in the ever-changing drummer's song.

About the Author

Doris Schneider

I am retired after teaching theatre at William Carey University for 6 years and North Carolina Central University for 27 years. Harcourt-Brace published my text *The Art and Craft of Stage Management*.

I have published 2 novels and one children's story: *Borrowed Things*, *By Way of Water*, and "Nana and the 'c.'" All of the titles can be found on Amazon.

In the reporters' box at a high school stadium, I was helping my daughter take care of the guest jurors at a band competition when the idea of this novel came to me. My tall grandson was playing the bass drum and in front of him marched a diminutive girl, also playing the bass drum. I could picture the girl stopping and spinning, the stadium lights flashing on the metal of her drum. From that imagined moment, the characters of Bernie and Allie emerged. I had no idea how they would get to that scene or what might happen after. They had to lead me, to bring life to an unmapped and very unexpected story.

We live in the Blue Ridge Mountains in a log home. There is a willow chaise on the back porch that overlooks a robust creek. That's where I write while my husband, Jim Coke, raises rare and endangered wildflowers.

Acknowledgements

The idea for *Room Meant for Music* began taking shape first as a novella under the title *Drummer Girl*. The manuscript was put aside for a long time, before it was rethought and rewritten. An expanded story and new title evolved.

For his guidance and challenges in this evolution, I want to thank my editor Richard Krawiec of Jacar Press, who is also a poet, novelist, publisher, humanitarian, and friend. I am grateful to Natalie Eleanor Patterson for her excellent copy editing, and Daniel Krawiec of Sable Books for his artistic cover design and book formatting.

Thanks to Michael Colonnese of Long Leaf Press for his edit of the novella, *Drummer Girl*.

And finally, my sincere appreciation to the many friends and writers who read and provided feedback and support throughout the process: Diane Bryson, Donna Crowley, Eloise Currie, Dr. Michelle Curry, Judy Hickson, Sherry Hollister, Karlene Knebel, Eileen Lettick, Denise Marx, Rachel Victoria Mills, Alan Mobley, Jeffrey Phipps, Jessica Rhyne, Joseph Rhyne, and Dolly B. Wilson.

A special thanks to my youngest reader, Calla Lily Salvador, who provided valuable help with teenage dialogue as well as insightful responses to plot and characters.

www.ingramcontent.com/pod-product-compliance
Lightning Source LLC
Chambersburg PA
CBHW070929250626
47159CB00009B/3172